god-line.com

god-line.com

by

Anonymous

A Glass House Book

god-line.com

ISBN: 1-892737-36-1

Library of Congress Control Number: 2003104357

Published by Glass House Books
Glass House Books
Post Office Box 492177
Los Angeles, California 90049

www.glasshousebooks.com

Printed in the United States of America

A special thanks to all of you
around the world who took the time
to e-mail your questions.

Introduction

I sat down at my computer and logged onto the Internet. Another lonely night of looking into that screen of world-wide communications. A direct link to everything one could ever want. Access to all—and all at our fingertips.

Hmm, then why do I feel so…so nothing? And why do I keep on searching this, this *thing* every night? And *why* am I talking to myself? And why do I have so many questions? Ahhh. Questions—so many questions. And so few answers. Alright, enough talking. I'm on-line.

Let's see…where do I want to go? What do I want? How about…a good time. Everyone likes a good time, right? Alright, let's type good…g-o-d no wait a second, boy, I can't even spell tonight. God. Hmmm. God looks funny spelled in lower case. I wonder if God has His own web site? He should! Everyone else does. Ah, what the heck, let's see. Let's type in…god…god…what would God call His line? A direct line to God. Something like, the Bat-phone. The God-phone. God-line!

Yeah. G-o-d…dash…l-i-n-e…dot…com

www.god-line.com Enter.

Huh, well I'll be. Something's coming up. He does have a web site. I mean, there is a site. I wonder what this is gonna be. Hmmm, "Site under construction," written in about every language possible. So much for that.

I don't know why, but I just kept looking at the screen—which only said that there was indeed a web site, but not an active one.

I couldn't help it…ya know what I did? I put my cursor in the center of the screen anyway, and I double-clicked.

Whoa!!! What have we here?

Questions. And *answers*! From who? Wow!

Take a look. You have got to see this.

god-line.com

Enter

Female, 37, Jackson Hole, Wyoming:
Dear God, why do you intervene in some cases and not in others?

There is a parable about a man who went to Pakistan, and he was going to a place that made rugs. He came to a loom where somebody was working on a rug. And he looked at it, and it was *ugly*. It had all of these weird shapes and color combinations, and the strings were hanging all out of it; and it was just such a jumble and a mess. And the person wondered, "What kind of a rug is this?" And then he walked over to the other side of the loom…and *there* he saw a *beautiful pattern*, with all the colors and designs flowing together so beautifully. It was the most beautiful carpet he had ever seen.

The problem right now is people are on the wrong side of the loom.

You have to be patient.

One day I am going to take you all to the other

side of the loom. And then...you are going to praise Me for everything I have done and exactly how I have done it.

The tragedies you will recognize as the hand of Satan. But you will see that I have restrained him as often as I could and still allowed freedom and allowed you to see the consequences that come with sin.

If I did not intervene, you would see a hundred times more drunk driving accidents, you would see a hundred times more disease and other things. But I have brought it down to the least number possible...but for you to still see the horror of sin.

Think about all of the people on the roads. Think about all the people who are drunk, the people who are on drugs, the people who are too sleepy, the people who are distracted because they just dropped their sandwich down between their legs...the people who just had fights with their wives or husbands and they're so mad they can hardly spit. With all those things going on you should have a thousand times more accidents than you have. But you don't because I am there saving as many as possible while being true to My commitment to deal with sin and its results in a complete and permanent way.

An Atheist, Montreal, Canada:
God, I don't believe in you. Prove me wrong!

Ha, ha, ha, ha... Yes, that is my answer. Just as

the scripture says, "God laughed in His heaven." Ha, ha, ha.

When Jesus was on trial and he was sent to Herod...Pilot didn't want to deal with Him, so he sent Jesus to Herod to force Herod to make the decision...to get Pilot off the hook. Anyway, when Jesus was on trial before Herod, Herod asked Jesus to do a miracle for him. Herod said, "If You perform a miracle, then we will believe."

And...Jesus didn't do a miracle. He wouldn't do it because Herod, as well as the other people present, had *plenty* of opportunities to see Jesus already in action. Jesus said, "I do everything openly. I've not done anything in secret."

There were opportunities for the people to see Jesus work miracles, even raise people up from the dead. So there was no further need to do a miracle because there were already enough miracles if they were just willing to open their eyes.

So...I've already proven My existence to you—if you just *open your eyes*.

Female, 30s, Songwriter, Nashville, Tennessee:

Dear God,

If You know the actions and the intents of all people, why let them live out their whole lives? If You know that some little punk kid is going to grow up to be a Hitler, for instance, why let him become that Hitler, knowing the consequences?

The answer to that goes back to the original Hitler, which is Satan himself.

I knew what his choices would be and that he would lead not only himself, but angels *and* human beings, into the terrible mess that we have now. And yet, I value freedom so highly that I would rather go to the Cross than to reduce the freedom of My intelligent creatures to any extent.

When you think about it, when Satan began to be selfish and headed toward rebellion, I had a couple of choices to make about how to deal with him. I could have just let Lucifer perish at that time, just withdraw My life support from Lucifer, and he would have died. Just as surely as if you had a computer that could be given the power of choice as to whether or not it's plugged into its electrical outlet; if it chose to unplug itself, then it would go out. And if I had allowed Satan, known as Lucifer at that time, to perish quickly as a result of his selfish choices and his rebellion, the other angels would have wondered where Lucifer was. And then the answer I would have given, because I tell the truth, I would have to have said, Lucifer is gone. "And why?" Well, because he started to think wrong things. "Oh, could that happen to us?" the angels would ask. Well, yes, it could. Well then, serving God out of love goes right out the window. And serving out of *fear* replaces it.

And, I could have just let Lucifer do whatever he wanted, and have no limits to what he could do at all. And that would just have caused *untold* misery and trouble for many more than if I were to restrain him in some way. I could have made a prison for Satan and put him in there...but that's not really valuing freedom, and that doesn't do a whole lot of good. Satan would be miserable and people would wonder, because he had been such a respected angel, why God would have done that, too. So even that would result in fear, because if he was in jail, "Could I end up in jail too?" Yes, according to this plan if you think the wrong thoughts you could end up in jail, too. So it's still back to fear.

And there's another alternative. I could have pulled the plug, so to speak, on Satan, and allowed him to perish, and then, *taken the memory* of Lucifer from every other intelligent creature...so that all the angels and anyone else would not even *ask* where Lucifer was, because they wouldn't remember that there was a Lucifer. So, since they wouldn't ask about him, there wouldn't be questions, no doubts, no suspicions, and therefore, no fear. Then everybody would just go along happily serving Me, and obeying Me, and worshipping Me, and everything would be just as beautiful and unspoiled as it was before...and nobody would know anything had happened—except, *I would know*. And what would I know? Well, I would know that I had taken that memory of Lucifer from My creatures *without* their permission. In other words, I would've treated them like robots. Robots are computers, and if you don't like what information is in them, you just take it out. You don't ask permission, because it's just a *thing*. And so, I would've been reducing their freedom, not very much, I mean, they wouldn't even be aware of it...it would just be a tiny bit that I would have been treating them without freedom. But what you find, is, that I would rather go through all the suffering that I've had to endure for all this time. And I've had to endure it more than anyone else—even more than a parent does with his or her child. And when a parent has a child that suffers...that *parent* certainly suffers with the child, sometimes even more than the child does. And so, I have suffered *more* than the people have. And, why? *Because I wouldn't reduce your freedom even by a teeny tiny bit.* And I have tried to treat you all as friends, equals, really. As much as I possibly can. You are finite and I am infinite...but I want to treat you as if you are My equal.

Not only do I know what the future holds—but I know *all possible futures.* So I know what would happen *if* I intervene in someone's life and try to make the future different than what the future was leaning towards. I know both situations—sort of like a chess player who has to think of about six or twelve different strategies...depending on how the other person reacts. I don't mean that I am playing with you, I am *interacting* with you while cherishing your freedom and seeking your best good.

Male, 32, Police Officer, LAPD, California:
Look, God, as you probably know, I beat a black kid last week. No one else witnessed it. (Except You, of course.) And I did not put this incident in my report. I truly feel that it was not because the kid was black. My explanation for what I did is—that you cannot run from a police officer and not expect a beating. That's just the way it is on the streets. Every punk knows that fact. If you run—when we catch you, it better not be on a back road or in an alley. If you run, you will get beaten. If you strike an officer, you will get beaten. If you raise any kind of weapon and point it toward an officer, you will get beaten, and a very good chance, shot! Point blank! And I'm not sorry for that. That's the job. I don't think I'll change. I can't change. I can't change and survive. What I have to ask You is: should I feel sorry or ashamed of how I handle my job? Am I being racist? And am I in a position where I should be asking for Your forgiveness? No one else's forgiveness, but Yours?

You need to look at *yourself* and see if you're a racist. That question deals with what's in your own heart. My question to you is—are you being honest?

In the Psalms, people were expressing a variety of things that were in their hearts.

David was once praying for his enemies—just like the criminals in the streets are often the enemy of the police. He's praying in verse 13, "But as for me, my prayers, O Lord, in the acceptable time, O

God, in the multitude of Your mercy here in the truth of Your salvation and deliver me out of the mire, let me not sink, let me be delivered from those who hate me and out of the deep waters."

Now, the mire can be interpreted as the mess, the dirt, the filth of the city that you are dealing with in your police work. You want to be a law enforcement officer and uphold the good of society, and what you're concerned about is not to be tainted by the bad of society. You don't want the mire to stick on you. You are not the first to be concerned about this. David was somewhat like My police officer. Back in the Old Testament he had to go and execute people, like the Amalekites for instance. Saul was told to go in and destroy them all, and Saul didn't do it, so later on David had to go in and clean up the mess that Saul left behind. Saul, by the way, who did not kill all the Amalekites, it was later an Amalekite who killed Saul. And then (about five-hundred years later) in the book of Ruth, there were still some Amalekites left, at least one, and he tried to work to lead the king of Persia to destroy *every* living Israelite, not just the king. So the sin that we do not destroy comes back and destroys us.

Now you are in Los Angeles, trying to uphold the law, and you don't want to be tainted by yourself or have the corruption creep into your own experiences, which would be in the form of overzealous violence, or racism, or things of that nature.

The way you can be kept clean is by staying in

connection with the goodness of God. The goodness of God cleanses your heart from the corruption of society. You can behold My goodness in My book, the Bible, and in My second book, nature.

You need to recognize that while it's good to hate evil, and to be ready to take action against those who are committing evil, you need to continually be honest with Me about your own heart and to recognize that evil can creep into your heart if you're not on guard and if you don't continue to allow Me to search you and to point out what needs to be corrected. If you are honest with Me, and you do like David did and turn to Me openly and honestly, I will deal with it. Just like a counselor, a counselor can't help a person be healed from anything unless the person is willing to be open and honest so that the counselor can *deal with it.* And that's what prayer is all about.

You may have heard the phrase, "Prayer does not bring God down to us—it brings us up to Him."

Male, 28, Minneapolis, Minnesota:
God, I've always heard that we are supposed to pray for others. But, how do we pray for someone that we may despise…like (Osama bin Laden)?

I believe that it's appropriate for Christians to pray for Osama bin Laden. Now, he may be *completely guilty* of being the person behind September 11th. But you can pray, first of all, that he be converted. You can be sure I would be interested in doing that because the Apostle Paul was originally the persecutor Saul, who killed scores of Christians simply for their faith in Me and yet I reached into his life and brought about his conversion and then he became a tremendous power for God's side. Certainly Osama bin Laden would be quite an influence if he became a converted Christian.

Also, Christians can pray that if Osama bin Laden refuses conversion, that God would intervene by allowing him and his associates to be blown up by their own bombs. And one of them recently was. One had a grenade in his car, ready to throw into an American Embassy, and the grenade went off in the car and killed the perpetrator rather than the intended victims.

You could pray that he be apprehended and receive just punishment.

Another thing as far as his conversion goes, you can pray that he and the others might try to pull off these different terrorist acts and everything *doesn't work.* In other words, they set the bomb, but the fuse doesn't work. They take the dynamite and they light the stick, and it goes out. They try to shoot the weapons, and the guns jam. *Everything* they try absolutely doesn't work...and then they start wondering what is going on here? And then pray that the Holy Spirit speaks to them and says, "I am God, and I'm not going to let you hurt these people. You need to turn to Me...and to Jesus Christ your Savior, and stop this foolishness."

Male, 33, Dublin, Ireland:
God, I am not going to say if I am a Catholic or a Protestant...but could you please tell me who is the right side to be fighting on? And when will the fighting end?

The fighting will end when you see that there *is no* right side to be fighting on. *Fighting* is the problem...not the people. Fighting, that's the problem. You have no enemy. Whether you're Protestant or Catholic. You don't have an enemy in your fellow human being. Your *enemy* is Satan...who's causing you to think that you need to fight and hurt your neighbor. You've got the wrong enemy. And the way you fight Satan is to put down your arms, and to, as the Bible says, *beat your swords into plowshares.*

Take the efforts that you're putting into war, and put them into helping others. If you're having a hard time with a neighbor, look for ways *to help* that neighbor. You will be amazed at how your *feelings* can change when you act on principle.

That's what I'm asking you to do, I'm asking you to consider My principles. I put them forth in the Ten Commandments, and then in the summary of the Ten Commandments, which is to love God with all your heart, and love your neighbor as yourself.

When Jesus was asked *who* is my neighbor, He told the story of the Jewish man who was out on the roadway and was attacked and left for dead. And when his fellow countrymen came by, people who should've felt a connection with him because he was one of them...but they just went right on their way. And the religious leaders, also, just went right along; they couldn't be bothered. But then, a Samaritan came along, which for you would be like if a Catholic Irishman were left for dead on the wayside, and a Protestant came along...and he was the one that not only stopped to help, but took him to the village and paid with his own money, for not only his lodging, but for his medical care, and food, and everything he would need, and promised to come back and *pay more* if needed.

And so, I say again, if you're slapped on the right cheek, turn the left. Not to be abused, but to say to your neighbor, *you're too important to me.* You're too important to me. I'm not going to run away—I'm going to stay right here. And I'm going to try to form a good relationship with you. And it doesn't matter if you have an attitude to hurt me—I want to help you.

You will be amazed at what can happen.

Female, 35, Secretary, Hays, Kansas:
Why is there so much tragedy in this world if God is a God of love?

Whenever you are puzzled about why I did do something or didn't do something, it is usually helpful to ask the opposite question.

For instance, if we go to the story about the flood in Noah's day, and you think about how I took the flood and destroyed thousands, yes, millions of people. And that *seems* rather harsh, that I would destroy so many and only save eight people. But the question is, first of all, did I really do that? Did I really save only eight people and destroy the others? Well, if you read the story you find out that I had sent Noah to preach to the people for a hundred years to come into the Ark. And I wanted *all of them* to be saved. And the Ark was big enough to have hundreds of people saved, at least. And then, if more had *responded*, I wouldn't have sent the flood.

The story of Jonah. Jonah went and preached in Nineveh; he said, "You people have been so wicked God is going to destroy this whole city. He's going to send fire down from heaven, and He's going to just wipe you out. In forty days, that's what's going to happen."

So Jonah preached that for forty days, and then he went outside the city and he watched to see the fireworks. But there weren't any! I did not destroy Nineveh after forty days. Why? Because the king led the entire city in repentance…and they turned from their wickedness. So when the people respond, *when enough people respond*, I change the whole plan.

And so, in the time of Noah…I could have changed the whole plan if there were too many people to fit into the Ark. I would have saved more if they would have responded…and they were given plenty of opportunities. I even lined up the animals and had them walk into the Ark. And the people *still* didn't believe enough that God was going to do the great thing that Noah had said would happen.

Can you imagine how startling it would be to see a line of wild animals just line up by themselves and go into the Ark? And yet the people still wouldn't respond.

So the thing to do is *ask the opposite question.* Instead of asking why would God destroy so many people, ask what would've happened if God *did not* destroy so many people? At that time the people were so wicked, their thoughts were constantly wicked, and they were full of violence...and so eventually they would have destroyed themselves *and* the eight people that I was saving. And then there wouldn't have been anyone left. So you can apply that question again and again to various experiences. Like when the people were in the wilderness and there was a group who rebelled against the leadership of Moses, I caused an earthquake that swallowed them up and destroyed them. Well, the question is, what would have happened if I *didn't* do that?

If you have a group of people who are under the direction of a leader...like a classroom. You've got a group of twenty-five or thirty seventh graders who have a teacher who's trying to lead them into knowledge...and if you have a couple of kids who are mouthing off to the teacher...and what if the teacher *does not* intervene with those students? Well, then the disrespect passes *all through* the classroom...*then how many* people learn anything? None.

So again the question is, what would happen if God didn't do anything?

Let's go back to the children who are abused, abducted, killed, and those kinds of things. What if I intervened in *every* case and saved every child? And what if I intervened in every car accident and nobody was killed, or if I intervened in every illness, so that nobody died of illness? And what if I intervened in every other kind of tragedy of life...so that people were saved in everything.

Let's say a man chooses to drink and drive, goes out and smashes his car into a tree...but I preserve him and save his life and the lives of anybody with him...and then nobody would ever get killed from a drunk driving accident...then, would you all feel that drunk driving was as bad as it is? You wouldn't see *the results* of drunk driving.

I told Adam and Eve in the beginning, "If you disobey me, you will die. It will lead to tragedy, destruction, and death. Not only for yourselves, but for others."

If I never let that happen, you would never realize how terrible it is to go against Me and My law.

Now, what *is* My law? *It is the law of unselfish love.*

Jesus said, "All of the law is summed up in two things: *love God with all your heart*, and *love your neighbor as yourself.*"

To break that law of unselfish love is to invite the terrible results of pain, tragedy, and destruction. But you would never know that if I didn't let the pain and tragedy and destruction happen. And you would think you could go on your way, be selfish, be proud, and do all the things Satan chose to do. You would feel you could just go right along as if there was no real problem. And why should I, in the end, allow the destruction of those who are disobedient to the law of unselfish love, if there's no terrible consequences. If it's not so bad, then why destroy them? And if it's not so bad...then why kick Satan out of heaven?

Love demands that sin and tragedy and death be dealt with, not just in a temporary way, but in a complete and permanent way. That is just what I am doing.

Male, 44, Retail Sales, Chicago, Illinois:
God, I'm a black man with a black question. What color are You?

Just the right color. Ha, ha, ha.

But to give you something more...in Paul's writings in Ephesians, he says, "Now in Christ there is neither Jew nor Gentile, male nor female, bond nor slave." And you could add, black or white, red or yellow.

It is also said that man was made out of clay. Well, what color is clay? It depends on where you are.

Female, 37, Flight Attendant, San Diego, CA:
Hello God, thanks for being there. I like my job, and I have for over 14 years now. But hardly a flight goes by without me having a moment of intense fear of a high-jacking. Sometimes I have to go into the plane's bathroom to recompose myself. Other times it hits me before I even leave my home. I enjoy my work, or rather have enjoyed my work, too much to give into this fear. I struggle with it, but it is still there. Can you help me with this? What can I do?

Fear is not always a bad thing.

In the book of Proverbs it says, "The fear of the Lord is the beginning of wisdom."

And in Revelation 14, verses 6 and 7, there is a message going to all the world that says, "Fear God and give Him glory for the hour of His judgment has come."

And so, fear is not always a bad thing. It certainly *can* be. That's why I said in First John, chapter 4, that perfect love casts out all fear. Now, there, I'm referring especially to the idea that people would be afraid of Me. The text says that fear has to do with punishment and often people think that they should be afraid of Me because I'm going to punish everybody who doesn't do what I tell them to do. That is a warped presentation of what is true. The truth is that I want everyone to have life, and I want to be able to bless and bring happiness to everyone. However, those who don't trust Me and My ways are going to go the other way, of course, and those are the ways of misery and death, so they end up with misery and death as a consequence of what they've chosen. When they discover that all of My dealings with them come from a motivation of love and that I will never hurt them and I will never point them in the direction of harm and death, then they see that they can trust Me; they don't have to be afraid of Me anymore. So, the understanding of My perfect love, My *reliable* love helps them to see they don't ever have to be afraid of Me...that I'll never hurt them or allow them to be hurt if they trust Me; at least not hurt in the big picture of things. I do allow hurts that are temporary and that are a part of attaining a big picture that is good.

Now, as far as fear of the terrorist... Why be afraid of the terrorist? Well, because they can bring about death. Why be afraid of death? Well, because death means the end of life. Why be afraid that life is going to end? Well, because maybe you're not ready to understand or trust what comes *after* the end of life.

If you know Me well, you know that My love has prompted Me to *prepare* for your death. Death is not the end. Those who understand the love that I've shown through Jesus will understand that eternal life is available. Just as John 3:16 says, "I so loved the world that I've given My only begotten Son that whoever believes in Him should not perish...(in other words, death is not the end) should not perish but have everlasting life."

So, I would encourage you to make sure that you believe in Jesus as your personal Savior and settle this issue as to what's going to happen to you after death. And then you don't have to be afraid of losing out on life, because the end of life as it is now is not the end of life for you, if you trust in Me and the salvation that I've provided in Jesus. And *that* only takes a moment to do—you just need to put your trust in Me and then keep doing that every moment afterwards, and you can be ready for death at any time it comes.

However, I understand that you may still be afraid of death because you recognize it would cut you off from your children, or your husband, or your parents, or your siblings, or some other loved one. You know that the loved ones left behind would suffer because of losing you, because of your death. And especially if it were in a tragic means such as a terrorist act. So, you may be thinking about that. Well, again, the answer to your problem is *perfect love.* Again, look to Me and understand that I'm big enough to care for all of those loved ones, and that I have perfect love *for them* as well as for you. If I allow a terrorist to act and your death takes place, I can go on caring for your loved ones. And when any problems arise for them I will have solutions. I can intervene for them. The important thing is that they would learn to know Me and to trust Me. While you are still alive you can help with that by praying for them and by showing My love to them…and that can help in a long ways toward their experience of fully trusting Me and claiming that gift of salvation that I've provided for them.

Then, if you trust Me yourself, and trust Me for your loved ones, then you can have a *peace* that the world can't give and can't even understand. Even in the midst of terror, you can trust Me just as Jesus did when He went to His trial. At death *He* was surrounded by terrorists, and yet, He had a peace and a nobility that no one could understand. And...that's available for you. It's available as you need it. You can have it—you can have it everyday. And you can portray the power of My love to stand strong in the midst of terror in a similar way as Jesus did. And the world needs that testimony right now. It needs it very much.

Concerned Mother, 34, North Star, Michigan:
Hello God,
It's good to talk to you. I feel sad though. God, what happens to the souls of all these missing abducted children across America...the ones that are never found?

There are two problems with your question. One is you've misunderstood what a soul is. In Genesis it says that when God made the first person He formed Adam of the dust of the ground and He breathed into him the breath of life and man became a living soul. It does not say that God put a living soul into the person. Man *became* a living soul. A living soul is a combination of two things: the dust of the ground and the breath of life.

In Ecclesiastes, chapter 12, it says that when a person dies the body goes back to the ground and the breath of life goes back to God who gave it to him. So, at death, if these children have died, at death they cease to be living souls. There are no living souls. It's like a wooden table...before a person makes the table there is only a pile of wood and a pile of screws...he doesn't have a table yet. But, when he puts the wood and screws together he has a table. But if he takes the screws out of the table and puts the pile of screws to one side and puts the pile of wood on the other side, where's the table? Well, there is no table...at that time. There is only a table when it's put back together. And that's what I can do and *will do* at the resurrection. I will put the breath of life back with the dust of the ground...and then you will have a living person again.

So, any of these children that have died or who are lost, they do not really exist until Jesus comes again and calls them back to life.

Before we go further, the other part of the problem with the original question is that you suggested that nobody knows where these children are. Well, *I* certainly know where these children are...and the guardian angels certainly know where the children are.

It says back in Psalms, 139, "Where can I go to flee from Your presence? If I go up to heaven you are there. If I go to hell, or the grave, You are there. If I go all the way to the other side of the ocean, You are still there."

And so it doesn't matter where a person goes, where the children are, I am watching over them, and I am with them...and the angels are with them.

Jesus loved the children in a special way. He said, "Let the children come to me and don't forbid them for of such is the Kingdom of heaven. And if you want to enter the Kingdom of heaven you have to *become* like a little child."

While they are alive, I am watching over them. When they die, they cease to exist as living souls. That doesn't mean they cease to exist all together because *I can still preserve their identities*. You don't need to know how, just know that I can.

Female, 39, News Broadcaster, New York, NY:

Dear God,

I feel obligated to be direct with you. As a news broadcaster for one of the top three cable news shows, I report to the world—which you know. My problem is—I know that I don't always report the truth. I don't want to make waves at work or with the network, but I have a problem with these feelings of being deceitful. People higher up than me make the calls as to what story goes out over the airways. Sometimes the story is presented in such a way as to lean towards the higher-ups' political leanings. Other times the story is partially fabricated for shock value. How can I do my job and be more honest at the same time?

Jesus said, "I am the way, the truth, and the life. The truth will set you free."

What's more important to you, your job or truth? What's more important—pleasing your boss and being liked by people, or having integrity?

Sometimes I can use you in a place that is less than what you might consider ideal.

What happened with Joseph might be helpful. Joseph was born into a family of faith, of Abraham's descendants, the family of Jacob, but he ended up down in the big city, in Egypt. His big break came when he was in Pharoah's court as the number two person in the whole Empire. There, he could not do things that he could do if he were a leader back in Israel, because there he would have the whole environment of all who are worshipping God and who have the same priorities of truth. But in Egypt he had to serve the Pharoah and whatever he told him to do. However, he did have a reputation for righteousness, so the Pharoah trusted him with some things beyond what he would trust others with.

The challenge for you could be to do everything you can to gain a reputation of integrity—integrity not just in dealing with the news, but a *personal integrity* dealing with situations in the work place. So much so that the bosses can see that they can trust you, that you are going to be consistent with your principles, that you will be a person of principle and you will follow those principles no matter what. So, when they have a call to make regarding the news, they ask for your input on the choices.

The same thing happened in the story of Nehemiah. Nehemiah was the cup bearer for the king, so he had to do whatever the king of Persia asked. And it was again, not an ideal situation. Nehemiah wished that he was back in Jerusalem, but that wasn't possible at the time. However, he had gained such a rapport with the king—through his personal integrity, and not only his integrity, but also with his daily attitude. The king noticed when Nehemiah was down in spirits because he was usually very positive, helpful, reliable and everything else. And the king said, "Hey, what's wrong with you?" And then Nehemiah got a chance to tell him about his concern for Israel...and then the king ended up sending the Israelites back to take care of the problem. So his *daily demeanor* made all the difference in My ability to use Nehemiah to change the course of history.

Single Mother, 35, Lynn, Massachusetts:
Hello God, how are ya? My question is — what is the purpose of life when we are all defeated (by death) in the end? Thanks.

Oh... That doesn't sound like a "Hello, how are ya?" kind of question. Ha, ha.

What is the purpose of life when we are all defeated by death?

I just need to think of the right wording. This is

an important question. The *wording* is...stimulating.

You have missed one of the most important things I've been trying to tell you. Your statement or question makes Me feel as if I failed at what I tried to do when I came to Earth, in Jesus. Because one of the greatest aspects of My mission was to defeat death *for you.*

When I went to the Cross, I was going to the Cross to take that defeat of death *away* from you. Truly, because Adam and Eve chose to involve themselves in sin, and *all* have sinned and come short of the glory of God, and the wages of sin are death...truly, humanity was under the pale or the burden of death. And, *that* truly would be a defeat. However, when I came and took humanity upon Myself, I carried weak, fallen humanity *with* Me through a life of perfect obedience that undid everything that Adam and Eve and the rest of humanity had done with their sins. And I lived, here in this world of darkness and selfishness, a perfect life, with *unspoiled, unstained, unselfish love.* And then, I went to the Cross and *gave My very life,* so that humanity could *live* and have *eternal life.*

As John 3:16 says, "For God so loved the world, that He gave His only begotten Son, that whosoever believeth in him should not perish, but have everlasting life."

And so this is a *free gift*...that's *for everyone.*

I died for the sins *of the world,* not just a few people. But really, everyone was saved. *All* of humanity was saved at the Cross. It's just that I don't force you to *accept* that salvation...I don't force you receive that *free gift* of life. And unfortunately, many of you refuse it. But please know that I died for you, and that the defeat that death would bring needs not come to you...and that you can be among those that I spoke of in John 11, when I was talking to Mary and Martha, and said that whoever believes in Me *never really dies*, that the death that comes to them is only a short sleep and then *I return* and *call you back to life*. And, it's like an *instant* has gone by, no matter how long the person is dead. And now you come forth to a life that is not only new, but is free from sin, discouragement, suffering, pain, and from ever dying again. Then you'll have an eternity of joy, love, fulfillment, growing, and security...a life I always wanted you to have. So please, don't, don't feel stuck and defeated. And when you realize how much I, not only have to offer, but how much I paid for you, and what a great price I've paid...oh, there *is* meaning to life. And not only that *you* have this gift of life, but you have the opportunity to be used *by* Me to help others discover this great gift.

<u>Male, Rock Star, London, England:</u>
Hi, God. I'm in my 50s now. Late 50s. I've done just about everything. When I drive down any street in any city I hear one of my songs on the radio. I'm known around the world. I was even called a god myself when I was younger...a rock god. I've seen a lot, man. But at times,

most of the time, I feel I haven't done anything with my life. I feel lost. Empty. My mates wouldn't believe me, but I don't know if I've ever been happy. My question is… what is the meaning of life?

There was a king named Manassah. He was a king in Judah, a southern kingdom in Israel. He was a king who left the faith of Israel and he started worshipping other gods and got involved in all kinds of ungodly things—from heathen parties to even sacrificing his own children to the gods, which, I believe rock stars have done—encouraging young people to sacrifice themselves to the gods of this world. I hope that's not too blunt for you.

So here was this king…and he didn't live this way for five years, or ten years, or twenty, or for forty; he did it for fifty-five years. From the age of twelve, when he took over the throne, till the age of sixty-seven.

And then, the Syrian Army came and overthrew him and his army and they put hooks through the king's nose and they led him through the countryside back to their prison. They imprisoned him. And while he was there in prison, he finally turned to Me. And he said, "God, I have blown it. It's true…what You have told me through the prophets, whom I have killed, one after another. I have ignored You, but now I see that I need You. I need You to deliver me from this."

And Manassah *was* delivered. He was sent home

and continued as king. He had to send money to Syria, but at least he was alive, and he was home. Then he said, "God, before I had *heard* about You, but *now I know* that You are God...and You alone will I worship."

Then he tried to undo all of the false worship that he had previously done. Now, it was kind of late in his life, and there were a lot of people in the country that he could not convince to get away from these false gods and false worship. But at least he tried the best he could with the little bit of life he had left. And he was accepted by Me and forgiven, and he *now* had some meaning in life. Finally.

Before, it was just partying, messing around, and being a bad influence...and he had thought that was cool. But when he got into a dire situation, where there *really* was a life and death problem, *then* he recognized that only God had the answers, only God could help him. I did help him, therefore, he knew that I could forgive him. He accepted that, and then he tried to undo the mess that he had been making all those years. And it did help some, but it couldn't turn around everything, unfortunately.

Now, what is the meaning of life? Well, certainly there's more than partying and making music. Life is something that's passed on from generation to generation. The gift of life was given to Adam. The breath of life was breathed into him. And that life has been passed from parent to child all through the times. And now the question is—are you passing on something that leads to life...or are you influencing people toward death?

The meaning of life is to encourage life.

Because while you are alive you have choices to make and you can choose those things that lead to addiction, despair, and suicide...or you can choose those things that lead to encouragement, uplifting, growth, and reaching potentials. Like Jesus said, "I have come that you may have life and life more abundant."

I don't want you to just have life and to just have meaning of life, I want you all to have *abundant* life.

You've asked the wrong question. You've asked the question, "What is the meaning of life," but your question should be, "What is the meaning of *abundant life*?"

Abundant life can be demonstrated in Jesus. What did He do? He spent his life—the potential he had, the time he had, the energies he had—*to help others.* Whether it was healing, whether it was teaching, whether it was lifting up the discouraged...whether it was calling a dead person back to life, giving sight to the blind, giving spiritual sight to the spiritually blind. All those things helped people have fewer burdens and greater joy.

<u>Male, 17, Mexico City, Mexico:</u>
God, I have a question. Many times there are reports and sightings of Guadalupe or the Virgin Mary in different objects around the world. Is that real? Are the visions real?

Perhaps you're asking the wrong question—are the visions *real*? Many things are real that are not good or from the source of goodness.

The visions and miracles can be real, but that doesn't prove that they are of divine origin.

Jesus said, in Matthew 24, that you can expect there to be false prophets and even false Christs.

In Revelation it says these people will be able to create miracles, wonders, and signs. So, just because a supernatural event can take place, and *really* take place, doesn't mean that it is something from Me.

In Deuteronomy, chapter 13, verses 1 through 5, it decries a situation where a person comes bearing a message from God. And the person performs a sign or wonder...and it actually takes place. And he makes a prediction and the prediction comes to pass. But then, that person leads the people away from the true God. And it says there, if that happens, do not follow that person because the Lord is testing you to see whether you *love* Him or not.

I wanted to know whether or not you love the real picture of Me...the *true* picture of Me that I have presented in My word.

In other words, say that the person working miracles encourages people to go after riches, and says that God is going to bless them with riches if they will follow this miracle worker. Then, what that does is encourage people to be greedy and implies that God's focus is on material blessings. And that's *not* the God of the Bible. Because you see Jesus on

Earth working with people, and not working through greed at all, *not* working with the material physical blessings of this world and putting emphasis on them. All of the talk that Jesus gave in regard to material things was merely to help the people recognize how much God loves them and cares for them, and that His purposes for them are *higher* than just the things of this world.

In Matthew, chapter 6, verses 20 to 33, talks a lot about that...where Jesus says so many people are always concerned about what they're going to eat, what they're going to wear, and what kind of place they're going to live in. But you shouldn't be that way because you know that your Heavenly Father is watching over you...more than He even watches over the birds and all the creatures, and if He provides for them, certainly, He is going to provide for you. So don't worry about it...just put the things of God first. Put God and His righteousness first.

So, if a person has been learning about the righteousness of God: His unselfishness, the pure principles of His Kingdom, the unselfish love, the purity and honesty, and nobility that Jesus represents...and that *those* are the important issues for God, then, if someone comes and paints a different picture of God, and even if they can *do* all the miracles and truly perform these supernatural events, *that doesn't matter*. Because they are painting an incorrect picture of God. Even if they use the word for God, like *Jesus*, and *God the Father*, and all of those *words* for God, but if they are painting a different picture of God, then there is a problem. And in the world today there are many who are going after these miracles of the Virgin Mary and many other things connected with that, Guadalupe, and so on. And yet, the institution, the church institution, that's connected with these things *does not* paint a picture of God that's consistent with the scripture. Because the theology that's presented causes people to depend upon the Church and the Priests, and the Church and the Priests *take the place of* Jesus. And that's *not* the way I intended it. I intended for people to come *directly* to Me. In their theology, God becomes *removed*, and you need layers of intercessors, between a sinner and God. Whereas in the scriptures, God reaches *directly* down into the life and heart of the sinner...and calls that sinner with His everlasting love to Himself. And no intercessors are needed. God Himself is His own intercessor when He reaches out for someone.

So don't be fooled by the supernatural; there'll be all kinds of *things*. Revelation says they can even cause fire to come down from heaven. But that's *not* the last word, that's not the ultimate confirmation that something's from Me. Even if somebody could raise people from the dead, that's not absolute confirmation because Satan can appear to be whatever he wants. He and his host could *pretend* to be the raised person. Let's say somebody, some miracle worker, went to Arlington National Cemetery where

President Kennedy is buried, and they went and *raised up* President Kennedy from the dead. And he came forth. And his brother Ted Kennedy was there and said, "I'm going to test to see whether this really is my brother. We had a secret when we were ten years old and no one else knows it." And he asks him the question, and that resurrected President Kennedy gives the correct answer. That *still* does not prove it, because Satan and his angels know all the secrets; they observe all activity and they can have that answer. And so that even would not be proof that that individual, that miracle worker, is from Me. The *proof* that I give you is found in Isaiah 8:20, where it says they have to agree with the scriptures. They have to agree with the Bible. And everything they teach and do has to agree with the Bible.

And then in Matthew, chapter 7, verses 17 to 22, it says that a person like a prophet or a miracle worker...you have to see what kind of fruit they bear. In other words, their lives have to be Christ-like. And the followers who follow their teachings, their lives have to be Christ-like.

So the teachings have to agree with the scriptures, and the results of the lives of the teacher and of his followers have to agree with the parable of Jesus...*then* you know that they pass the test of scripture and can be accepted as truly from Me.

In Matthew 24, where Jesus warns about false Christs and false profits, He says that people will say, "Behold, He is in the desert, or He is in a secret place...but do not go out."

There is much opportunity in the world for Satan to deceive people. And if people perhaps look at this remarkable thing in a tree or on the wall of this building, there is this *stain* that looks like the Virgin Mary...just because these things happen and people jump to the conclusion that it is the Virgin Mary—it must be important, it must be very important—because all these miracles are happening with Virgin Mary...that's *not* the proof, because Satan may want to exalt the Virgin Mary for *his own* purposes.

In the Old Testament, for instance, there was a time when I directed Moses to make a brass serpent and hold it up because they were being bitten by these serpents in the wilderness. And My command was if they *look* at the brass serpent that he provided, they would live. If they didn't, they would die. So that's what happened, the people who looked lived. So they kept that brass serpent through the years, and many years later there was a group of people in Israel who began to *worship* the brass serpent. So there's a tendency in humanity to worship the wrong things. Even though something is very good for one purpose, I don't mean for it to be worshipped. And the Virgin Mary, even though she was a good person, and she fit into My plan in a wonderful way and was a good example of faith and obedience to Me, the Bible never exalts her as someone to be worshipped, or someone who was a co-redeemer with Jesus, or someone who is alive in heaven with some kind of an intercessory ministry for you. That's never mentioned. There is not anything of that in the scriptures. And so you mustn't jump to the conclusion based upon things *outside* of the scriptures. And that brass serpent...it had to be destroyed, so that the people wouldn't worship it.

So if you hear of some sign or wonder—then don't worry about it. Just let it be. It doesn't mean you have to run out and follow it. Because Jesus said, "*Don't* go out." When people say, "God's doing something in the wilderness. He's doing something over here. He's doing something over there." Don't run around after that. Instead, go back to the Bible, and look for what the Bible has to say about that thing. Stay close to My Word. Because, as the Psalmist said, "Thy word is the lamp under my feet and the light under my path."

Go where the Bible directs you to go—not where the supernatural directs you to go.

<u>Male, 21, Penn State College Student, Pennsylvania:</u> God, what religious study should I read? The Koran, the Bible, the Talmud, the Book of Mormon? What do you really suggest?

The one that sets itself apart from all the others. And you figure it out. Ha, ha, ha.

In Isaiah, Chapter 48...the people had a problem in Isaiah's day, mostly with idols, and so I challenged them, and I said, "Who is going to compare to Me? You think that the other Gods are just as good as Me and you can worship them as well as Me? So let's compare—just try to compare somebody to Me."

Who can tell the future? I can tell you from the beginning what's going to happen, all the way to the end. There is absolutely *no other God* who can do that. And so, when you're looking for My book, then what should you expect *it* to set itself apart with? Since I said I set Myself apart with the ability to foretell the future...then you can expect that My book will set itself apart with its ability to foretell the future.

When you look at the prophecies of Daniel, especially, you can see very clearly the Bible foretelling the future accurately. In Chapters 2, 7, and 8, it mentions kingdoms that would come, and the order in which they would come, and *names* them by names. And they came in *exactly* that order. And only the number I said would come. And then there would be a division. And then, Europe happened at that time, the divided nations of Europe after the fall of the Roman Empire. And you have not seen another Roman Empire. It also says that the nation would try to pull together to form another great empire, and they would even try to intermarry to make that happen. And history reveals that's *exactly* what happened...but they could never *make* that happen. Hitler tried to make it happen, Charlemagne tried to make it happen, Napoleon tried to make it happen, but nobody could *make* it happen. Even *com-*

munism could not make it happen. There has never been another great empire and there *never will* be another great empire...until I set up My Kingdom on Earth.

Also in the book of Isaiah, two hundred years ahead of time, I foretold the king of Persia would come and deliver the people of Israel from their bondage and send them back to their land to reestablish the kingdom. And the Bible mentioned Cyrus, *by name,* two hundred years before he even existed. And that was fulfilled precisely as well.

The book of Daniel also talks about the coming of Jesus; it gives the exact year when Jesus would arrive and the exact year when He would die, for others. And He came and He died exactly on time.

And so the Bible doesn't ask you to believe it just because it *says* that it's inspired—the way the other books do—it *sets itself apart* from all the others. There's no other book that can do that.

Male, 51, Defense Attorney, Los Angeles, CA:

Hello God. It's been a while since we've talked. You're aware of what I do for a living. And I know that You are aware of the fact that I have never felt bad for the work that I do and the position that I take for the client's interest. But in the years since we've last talked, I have represented some pretty unsavory characters. I questioned the innocence of some of them, but I didn't ask or bring it up with them. Some I thought were more than likely guilty, but I didn't comment or ask. And yes, a few of them, one in particular, I actually felt that he was guilty. I still represented him...and he was acquitted. I am now asking for help, God. What I am dealing with is the after effects of defending a killer. Am I wrong for what I do? I didn't used to think so. I used to like what I do. Used to. In any event, thanks for Your time.

One of the things that comes to mind is that *I* designed a legal or *justice* system. Now, you have a judge who is guiding the court so that everything is kept on the up and up, and the jury is able to make a good decision based on good facts, and then there's the prosecuting attorney who is bringing the charges...and then, there's the defense attorney.

In the Old Testament, in the guidelines that I gave to the people, there was no defense attorney. The judge was the defense attorney...or, the judge did that work. The judge was the one to defend the accused to make sure that every possibility of not only a fair trial, but that every bit of evidence on behalf of the accused was brought forward and considered by the jury. Which makes the picture of the judgment, My judgment of the world, an interesting one. Because with Me, you don't need any defense attorneys in life. Because I, Myself, as the judge, am also your defense attorney.

Jesus said, "The father judges no man but has given all judgment unto Me."

Jesus is called your advocate, or your defense lawyer. Jesus is both defense lawyer and judge. So, the judge is *on your side*, so to speak.

The scriptures portray Me as the One who will bring about *ultimate justice.* Right now you know that the world isn't fair. Things just aren't fair. And it has to be that way in order for the results of sin to be allowed, because *sin is unfair.* Sin not only hurts the person who chooses it, but it hurts innocent bystanders. And that's one reason why sin is so horrible and why I have to completely obliterate it from the universe. And anybody who holds onto it will have to be obliterated too. That's a horrible thing...in fact, in the Bible it's called *God's strange act.* But it has to be, because sin is such a destroyer, destroying the innocent along with the guilty. But one day I will bring about the final justice and it's going to be through the judgment process. But I use judgment, I don't only use force...I won't just stand up at the end and say, "Alright, everybody who's been on My side I'm going to save, and everybody who's against Me I'm going to destroy." I don't and I won't do that. Instead I go through a process of judgment where I open up the records for the onlooking universe to examine it, and to see how I have dealt with all different situations, how I have dealt with different people. In a sense, I am on trial *Myself*...in the judgment *more* than the people on trial.

Romans, chapter 3, verse 4, says, "God may You win Your case when You bring it into court."

Therefore, you see that I am extremely interested in *justice*.

Now, what you, Mr. Defense Attorney, are involved in is a system of justice. Of course, it's a man made system and therefore it's less than perfect. And it is still dealing with things in this world where things are less than perfect, where things are *unfair*. Sin and its consequences are being allowed to run their course. I don't expect people to only be interested in the justice system if they can be a part of perfect justice, because there really isn't any. But, the fact that you are trying to be true to the principles *of* a justice system, and although it is flawed, it is still one of the best that has ever been devised...a system that seeks to have real justice...where those who are truly guilty are punished and those who are innocent are *not* punished and are allowed to go free. And so by defending the criminal, whether guilty or innocent, you are being true to *principle*...and that is the principle of the justice system in which you are involved...and the society in which you live. And so you are thereby working toward a semblance of the justice that I am interested in.

In Romans 13, it talks about the obligation of the Christian to follow the laws of the land as best as he can, unless those laws contradict God's law. And I don't know of anything in the scriptures that says that you can't *defend* a guilty person.

Yes, sometimes it seems that there are possibilities for the guilty to not receive punishment, the punishment he deserves. Unfortunately, that is true. And it is a burden.

So bring that care, that concern, to Me and leave

it with Me…and then pray for that guilty party. You can pray, first of all, that now that he's released, I may intervene in his life and bring about his conversion so that he will no longer be a murderer. So that the man that is free will not be a murderer but he'll be a person of faith and a righteous person. And therefore you haven't gotten a murderer off, you've gotten a righteous person off. Secondly, you can pray that if the murderer *refuses* to be transformed by the grace of God then the murderer will be caught for something else for which he will be convicted and the punishment will come upon him. And you can pray that if the Lord chooses not to use the justice system to punish him that the Lord would punish him in some other way whether it be through an accident or the direct visitation of My destroying angel.

So, as to your feelings of guilt that a guilty murderer who was your client has now been released due to your skill, you need not hold onto that guilt, but rather release it. Let it go. Bring it to Me. The Bible says, "Cast all your care upon Him for He cares for you."

<u>Female, 15, H.S. Student, Dallas, Texas:</u>
Dear God, why don't we use all of our brain?

You don't use all of your brain *now*.

Today, if you go out and buy a computer, would you buy a computer that has the capacity to do just barely all that you want to do with it right now? Or would you buy a computer that has capacities to do *beyond* what you can do right now, beyond the kinds of programs you're interested in running right now? If you had the opportunity to have one, the means to buy it, and if it was available to you for purchase, would you choose something that could do a whole lot more *eventually*? And, of course, the implied answer is that most people who are knowledgeable and are used to using a computer would purchase one that has a lot more capacity than what they're using right now, because they realize that eventually they're going to want to *do more* than what they're doing now. They're going to learn more and be willing to expand their goals and have more up-to-date tools to use on the computer, willing to get into more complicated programs and so on. Therefore, they'll accomplish more in their lives or their work or personal interests.

The same way…when I created Adam and Eve; I created them with a huge amount of mental capacity. Because, I intended them to learn not just from what was in the Garden (the things that could be learned with their short time), but I expected and *planned* for them to be able to continue learning, not only through a life span of seventy or eighty or ninety years or even a life span of nine-hundred years, as they lived originally, but, I planned for them to go on living forever. That's why I put the tree of life there in the Garden, not just the tree of knowledge of good and evil. I planned for them to be able to enjoy living and growing and developing their mental abilities, and their understanding of Me and the universe, and to continue growing and developing throughout eternity. And that's what I planned for you, as well. I really want you to know Me and I want you to understand what I have done, what I am doing now, and what I am going to do in the future. I want you to understand the principles behind all of that. I want you to understand others and their perspectives in this world, in relationship to Me...the problems of sin and all...and I want you to understand the other worlds, too, and what *they* have seen. I want you to understand the angels, and what they have been through.

There's a *whole lot* for you to learn. It's going to take a long time. But, it's going to be a good time. It's going to be you and Me together. And, we're going to enjoy it a lot. So, I'm glad you have the capacity to take that journey with Me. I look forward to it.

Male, 24, Muslim, New Jersey:
If you are God, I tell you Allah is great! What do you think of that?

Why do you think so? What is so great about your picture of God, which you call Allah? Is he great in *power*? Is he great in his thirst for revenge? Is he great in *wisdom*? How about *kindness*? Or, is his kindness *not so great* because it's only kind to a few people, the ones who call him Allah? Is he great in *compassion* for those who don't yet know him…or those who have turned their backs on him? Is he great with *grace*? Does he desire to reach the worst sinner and *win him*, rather than seeking to punish him?

You need to stop and think about those questions.

Who is the greater God? What are the greater principles that He's operating from?

Some picture God as operating with the principles that Satan has chosen: the principle of force, the principle of exclusivity, of demand…where people have to reach up to Me to try to please Me. Instead of a very different picture of God, which is Me reaching down to those who have turned their backs on Me. A God who dies for people while they are yet sinners.

Is your God great in the *goal* that he has for each human being?

I want you all to become as much like Me as you can be.

I have heard some people call *you* a lousy radical Muslim. Well, I would like to take *you* and bring *you* to the place where *you* reflect the greatness of God.

In Exodus 32, Moses said to Me, "Show me your greatness, your glory."

And I passed by him…and Moses saw *kindness* and *patience* and *love*.

What Moses was shown is not an image of a being or a brightness and a majesty, but he was shown *character qualities*. And so the greatness of God is My character. That's why when Jesus was on Earth He could reveal the glory of God without revealing the shiny brightness that you can't approach because it's so tremendous. He could reveal the glory of God because He showed *the character of God.*

Female, 26, Artist, Venice, California:
Dear God. Does the sun think?

Ha, ha, ha. It would take an artist from California to ask that question.

Well, let's see what happens here.

There are several religions that have the understanding that God is in *everything*; that there's a piece of God in the flowers, there's a piece of God in the animals, in the trees, in the sky, in the sun, and so on. That God is in everything. Some people call this pantheism. The problem with that thinking is that it doesn't distinguish between Me and My creations. It would be like the artist who creates a painting. Now you might say that there is a part of that artist that is in the painting. And certainly, it was the talent, the thought, the emotion, and the personality of the artist that came out in the painting, that made the painting the way it is and different from anyone else's painting. And in that way that's true. But you wouldn't say that there's a *piece* of that person in the painting. The painting is *separate* from the person. And so, while the painting can *stimulate* thought and emotion in another intelligent being, we see the *separation* between the painting and the painter. It is similar between Me and My creation. I want every aspect of My creation to demonstrate some aspect of Myself, some part of My conviction and principles. I want My intelligent creatures, with the angels, unfallen beings of the universe, and especially the fallen beings on the planet Earth…I want them to be able to see aspects of My character. Because I operate on principles *always*—not on whim, not on emotion, not on pressure from others, not just on an urgency of the moment or the circumstances. I always act on principles. And My principles can be summed up, as Jesus said, in that great principle of *unselfish love*.

And I want people to see that…in the sun, and in the moon, the flowers, the trees, and the insects, and in *everything*.

Now, sin has entered into this world and marred that. There are now thorns on the roses, diseases in the bugs, and violence in the sky, with the hurricanes and so on. And so it's marred. My creation has been marred. The reflection of My character has been marred there. However, even with that, there *still* can be seen many aspects of My character, as well as My power, My creative power. And the intelligence of the design that I incorporated into *all* of creation.

And so the sun, though it itself does not think,

it's *not designed* by Me to think, it is designed by Me to shine, and to provide warmth, and light, and gravitational pull, and other things. But, hopefully *it* will cause *people* to think.

When the person who tends towards atheism studies how the Earth is in *exactly* the right place in its gravitational journey around the sun and is found at the right distance for life to develop (too close would be too hot, anything further would be too cold), and as they study the kind of light that comes from the sun, and what it's capable of doing to benefit life on Earth, and the atmosphere that I placed around Earth that protects from the harmful aspects of the sun, so that only the good can come through...all these things. I want people to see and recognize that there is a thoughtful creator who has the good of His creation in mind. And, that's...what I want. I want your good. And I want...I want you to think about Me when you see that good.

Female, 38, Oklahoma City, Oklahoma:
In a court of law, for a conviction of murder, is the death penalty right?

That's a good question from *Oklahoma City*.

Is the death penalty right in a court of law?

The question brings up two elements of love. And remember, you're asking Me, and as I've said in My Word, *I am love.* So I can't answer your question apart from love. But there are two parts to love, and sometimes humanity, you tend to get all caught up in one aspect or the other, and have a hard time blending them together.

The two aspects are: *justice* and *mercy*.

Sometimes when people read My book, they look in the Old Testament and they feel like they see only a God of justice, who's interested in *only* justice and has no mercy. They tend to see only the actions that are done to destroy people and to wipe out villages, and angels sent to kill tens of thousands, and armies, and so on, and they pick *that* out. And they look at the New Testament, and they think that that's only about mercy. They see Jesus dying for the sins of the world, and people being forgiven, and sins are forgiven and put aside...and all My mercy and kindness and sweetness...and they don't see the *blending*.

If they look really close at the Old Testament they would see that before I sent the justice, I pleaded with the people to not go there. Don't get into this mess, don't continue in disobedience and distrust and independence and rebellion, because it's going to lead to a *necessity* for severe action, for punishment, for the kind of discipline that you will only listen to, that *has* to be severe.

And in the New Testament, they don't see (or they don't want to see), the parts where I have to discipline *severely* at times. Now there is a good emphasis to help people see the mercy, because they've been looking at the justice for so long. So when Jesus came, He emphasized the mercy and the grace, and the love, and the tenderness. But there were also times like in Acts, chapter 5, where Annanias and Sapphira had to be severely disciplined. Yes, they were executed by Me…because of *lying*. Something many wouldn't have expected to *see* in the New Testament. But it was necessary. Justice and mercy have to go together, they have to be blended in the right way. Just like in a family. I love the elements of the human family, and Jesus often spoke of them in His parables. In a family, a wise and loving parent knows how to blend justice and mercy. Both are needed. There has to be discipline that is severe enough to get the attention of the child and to *direct* that child to the thing that needs to be learned, because there is so much in this world that is dangerous. And if the children don't learn within the security of the home the important lessons that will then protect them from the dangers that are outside the home, then, when they are on their own, they won't be ready and they will fall prey to untold danger. And so, this is what I'm trying to do with people through all times…especially with the nation of Israel where, at least some were willing to learn it…and then in the Christian church.

Now, when we come back to that *specific* question—of the death penalty—those who have read the Bible see that in The Old Testament the death penalty was part of the directions that I gave to the nation of Israel. As they went into the Promised Land this is how they were to operate…and part of it was the death penalty. If someone took a life, they had to give their life.

Now, in the courts today, the American judicial system, there are times when there is a blending of justice and mercy. There are those who want to emphasize the justice, there are those who want to emphasize the mercy. And, there are good reasons for emphasizing each side. The challenge is to know when to emphasize which. There are people who have *so* united themselves with evil, that the best thing is for them to be done away with. For those lives to end. Because there will be no good that will come from their lives. There are others who have united themselves with evil but at some point they might be willing to relinquish that stand and to turn to Me, and do good things, and their lives can change and be used for good. Even if their whole lives are going to be spent in prison, they can still be used for good *there*. And, of course, there are those who are innocent, who have been convicted of crimes that would be resulting in the death penalty who *shouldn't* be dying. And, that's part of the discussion as well.

And so I am going to leave you to wrestle with this. It's good for you. It's good for you to wrestle with these issues of *justice* and *mercy*. So I'm not going to answer that. If I answer that for your society, you will simply act based on that and not wrestle with the issues anymore, and just go on with life…without Me. And I want you to be thinking about *what I would want* and what My *principles* should lead to. And so, this is one thing that perhaps, will cause people to give more serious consideration to *what real love is*. And what it is composed of. And how it relates to real life. And how *I* relate to real life.

Female, 33, Lawyer, Sydney, Australia:
Dear God, why do people (men in particular) pass up good opportunities (me)?

Ever since sin entered this world, human beings have had a hard time really *seeing* the *value* of My creation. But especially My creation in regard to *people*.

As soon as Adam ate from the forbidden fruit, he lost his value for Eve. He didn't see her the same way. Instead of seeing her as someone he cherished and who had such great value in his eyes, that he would even give up his life for her...once he ate and joined her in sin, he then saw her as *a problem*, and an opportunity to get out of trouble. So when he was questioned by Me about why he ate from the fruit, he immediately said, "Well, *she* made me do it. This woman that You gave me, she's the one who got me in trouble. It was only because she brought it...that's the only reason I ate of it."

And so, Adam wasn't seeing Eve the same way, he wasn't seeing her value, and her beauty, and the wonder of her. He was thinking about himself. And that's the problem right on down through, people tend to think about themselves more than about others. And, unfortunately, the male part of the species tends to do that even more than the females in many regards.

I placed within woman the desire to please her husband. I mentioned, right there in Genesis 3, when I was talking to Adam and Eve and the Serpent, that the desire of the woman would be for her husband. And of course, for her children, she would feel bonded to them and have, generally, a great desire to care for and nurture them.

But the man, *his* great effort of life, is to succeed in providing for his family. So he is concerned about succeeding in work and being able to work hard and accomplishing things and solving problems. He just tends to get stuck in that, and selfishness *limits* what he can do...and so he gets focused on that, and it is all he's thinking about. He's concerned and focused on his *success* and *ability to provide*. His mind isn't opened, his faculties aren't trained to also take in the *value* of this family he's providing for, and the *value* of this wife that's by his side and the abilities that she has...her beauty, not just her outer beauty, certainly, but her inner beauty, and the wonder of what she can accomplish, what she can do that he can't...the insights that she can provide; often, men aren't seeing that.

The concern I'm hearing in your question is that you're being passed by. Don't forget, *I don't mind* you bringing that concern to me. I don't mind being involved in the match-making business.

If you go to the story of Isaac, when Abraham saw that it was time that Isaac needed a wife, Abraham sent his servant, Eliezer, to go back to their home country and find a good wife. Eliezer *trusted* Me, and so he invited Me to be part of it. And I was. And I led Eliezer to the right person. Rebecca was her name. Eliezer didn't just ask for some weird sign, but he asked for a sign of My leading that would indicate her character, that she was a person who was cheerful, helpful, hard working, hospitable, friendly, and giving. And so all of these good traits of character were involved and indicated by the kind of sign he asked for. *And I was glad* to be part of that. And I led, and Isaac and Rebecca loved each other and theirs was a great union. And so, I am glad to help. I am glad to be involved. If you will invite Me and trust Me, I will, just as much today as I did in the time of Isaac, lead you to the person who will appreciate you.

Now, you have to be willing to focus on My principles. And I am a stickler for good character. It's got to be a guy who has character and someone who will serve you well as a husband. There's the principle of true union. And that means a union not just based on the fact that you both like pickles on your hamburger, and the same kind of car, and the same kind of music; it's got to be a union that involves your real heart and soul and mind and your dreams. It's got to be someone who can share all of that...and who can be a husband and a leader of the family and a leader of your children that you can admire. So that means that you're going to have to be a stickler about principle as well. And that means you're also going to have to be patient. Because, I'm not going to *force* somebody to come to you. But I can *work* with people, and I can work with circumstances. If you will be patient, you will be amazed at what I can do for you.

Female, 39, Teacher, Greenville, Mississippi:
What is the point of all this? Why am I here?

You're here because *I want* you here. And I'm hoping that you'll let Me work things out for you so that you can be here *forever.*

But I know that your question goes beyond you as an individual. Your question seems to have in mind, why is *the whole world* here?

My plan for the world was made as part of a whole process I have in mind for the universe, especially the intelligent creatures in the universe. Together—Myself, and God the Son, and God the Holy Spirit—together We decided that it would be a good thing to create creatures who could truly think and feel and choose, creatures that were truly *free* and could *respond* to Us...in love, and appreciation, and enjoyment. And creatures whom We could please, to whom We could bring a sense of awe, and wonder, and joy. So We decided to create this kind of creature.

As We made the plans, We recognized that *freedom* would be such an important issue. True freedom...in order for them to be *as much like Us* as We could make them. However, We also recognized that with them being finite, and Us being infinite, that there would be such a vast difference between Us that it would be a hard thing to bridge. With them being truly free, the process of bridging that gap would take many steps. And so we created them—I'll call them *angels* to help you—We created the angels with intelligence and freedom and personality and the ability to think and question, and then We began to work with them, to teach them, and to unfold things about Ourselves to them. And the next step in unfolding to them, was the creation of this world. The planned step was that We would create a world where there would be sexuality. There would be male and female. And the male and the female could come together, and in their expression of love for one another, they would be involved in *creating* beings that would be in *their* image. So the angels looking onto this world would be able to *see* this *ability* to create out of love in your own image. And then to *love* that creature, that child, with all your heart. And then, that would give an insight to Us as God; that We create out of love and then We *love* who We create. And that would help the angels to grow with their understanding of Our abilities and Our character...and Our ways of doing things.

So that's what the world was planned for.

Now, before the plan could be enacted, Satan's rebellion interrupted things for a time. And then Satan's involvement has complicated things. However, I am not letting Satan have the last word. I am not letting sin destroy the plan. It's going to be dealt with; it's going to be dealt with completely and finally, as I explain in Revelation; I'm going to create the world anew. And I'm going to take the saved human beings and I am going to dwell with them, and My plan is going to be complete, because the universe will see that I truly do love and value freedom and individuality, and that I want to share *as much* of My abilities with My creatures as I possibly can…and still maintain their good in mind.

So *the point of all this*…will be accomplished as I complete My plans. And My point for *you* will be accomplished as well, if you let Me. Because Jesus has *won* the greatest battle in this whole thing. He won it at Calvary. And so *everyone* who joins with Him will come out on the good. They will be part of the final victory. And *you* can have the eternal life that I planned for everybody. You can have it, and you and I can enjoy eternity…together. And *that* is a very big point—to Me.

Male, 18, College Student, Encino, California:

Dear God,

I am a Jewish teenager, born and raised in the United States of America…Encino, California, to be exact. Encino is an alright place, but I am more proud of the fact that I am from the United States of America. I am second most proud of the fact that I am Jewish. I love my family, my friends, my religious background, and my freedom to pursue the life I choose. My question is — I want to go to Israel to study in their universities…to learn and experience life in my family's religious homeland. And to, in a way, serve Israel and support them during these incredible times. My problem—I mean my question is—that I have some fear. I hate to admit it, but even with all of the passion I have to go to Israel, I still have some fear for my life. I don't want to die. Not yet. Can You please help me? How can I get rid of my fear, yet maintain the passion?

Let me go to Joshua 1, verse 9, "Have I not commanded you to be strong and of good courage? Do not be afraid or dismayed for the Lord thy God is with you wherever you go."

And there's another verse in the Scriptures that says, "The Lord is with me, of whom then should I be afraid?"

Now, a question to *you* could be: If you believe that I would be with you in Israel, why do you believe that I would *want* you there? And if I want you there, then certainly I would be with you, and then you wouldn't have to be afraid of what man could do to you, for I can work in all things.

Romans, chapter 8, verse 28, "We know that all things work together for a good to those who love God and are called according to *His* purpose."

So if you feel called, if it's My purpose to go to Israel, if you love Me, then I am saying, I will go with you and you don't have to be afraid, because, *what can man do to you when I am with you?*

It's like David facing the giant, Goliath. Everyone else was afraid, but David was so upset with what Goliath was saying about Israel and their God, that to the other Israeli soldiers, he said, "Who is this *dog* to talk like this about the Lord God? Somebody give me a sword, I'll go over and take care of him."

So David was ready to go…he didn't stop to think twice, because he had such *a passion for My reputation.*

So why do you want to go to Israel—for My reputation? Or is it for the reputation of Israel alone? Is it for the reputation of the people and their heritage? If it's for your own purpose, then that's not enough. But if you have a passion for My reputation…ah, then that's a different story.

<u>Female, 30, Florist, Springfield, Missouri:</u>
Dear God — Recently someone discovered a stone box that is thought to be the burial box of "Jesus' brother." Did Jesus have a brother…and is it his burial box that they found or is it a hoax?

In the Bible, Jesus is portrayed as having, not only one brother, but a few brothers and sisters. But the one who is well known is James…who is considered to be the author of the Book of James or the letter of James. That is one of the Books of the Bible. He was also considered as the leader of the New Testament church. In Acts, chapter 15, when there was a disagreement on different segments of the church concerning some important issues, the church met together as a body to settle those issues, and James was the disciple, the leader, who was presiding. And, so, yes, Jesus did have a brother, here on Earth, and he did eventually die. In fact he was one of the first disciples to die. He wasn't the first Christian martyr, because Steven was that, but he was the first of the twelve disciples to die.

At that time, the person who died was embalmed, and then either put into a carved-out tomb, such as Jesus was, where there is no box involved, it's just a carved-out tomb, carved out of rock. Or, he would have been put into a poor person's common grave, which would just be a hole dug into the ground, with no box involved. So, according to what you know from history, this, would be a hoax, to claim this was the box that Jesus' brother was buried in.

Let us suppose that there were some exceptions wherein a box was used. This may be the box or it may not be. But really, what difference does it make? What are you looking for? Even if there was a box used, and, this was the very one from the brother of Jesus...what good would it do you? What good would it do you *to know* that this was the box? What good would the box do for you if you owned it, other than the fact that it would be a valuable piece of history, such as a piece of Noah's Ark? If somebody found Noah's Ark, and you had a piece of it, what do you think that would do for you? Do you think it would bring you good luck? Do you think it would connect you to My power? What value do you expect to have from this? People have considered this through the centuries.

There are churches that value pieces of wood claiming that they come from either a piece of the Cross that Jesus was crucified on, or a piece of the ship that Paul was shipwrecked on, or some other connection with a Bible personality or some famous Christian from history. Also, some churches collected bones...pieces of bone fragments that they believe came from this saint or that saint, disciple, or someone famous. The Muslims take long journeys to visit and touch the Kaaba stone, considering it to be a Holy stone set up by Abraham or Abraham's son, Ishmael. And other religions have other kinds of holy objects. But if you look in My Word, I try to help people understand that, for Me, *things* (objects, physical objects) are not important. I've tried to help My people through the ages understand that those things aren't the important things. It's *people* that are important to Me. And that's why when I created a temple...when *I* created a temple—and please, distinguish from the temple that I asked Moses and the people of Israel to make for Me in the wilderness, although they did make a physical temple—but when *I* made a temple, it was not a temple occupying space, or a temple with a physical building. I created a temple in *time*. It was the seventh day as a Sabbath day, a Holy day. A time where people, no matter where they were, no matter what country they were in or what language they spoke, or what their situation, they could enjoy My presence...in a day. Because, twenty-four hour days come to everyone. And so, that was meant to help people understand that *the person* is valuable to Me...and *time with that person* was something Holy.

So please, don't get side-tracked by boxes and bones and all of those objects. But come to Me, personally. I want to meet with you. I want to have some time with you. I want to get your attention and show you things you've never seen before.

Female, 38, Lima, Peru:
Dear God,
What is the future of mankind? Can You give us a hint?

Hah, *a hint*! I've told you the whole thing!

Well, I shouldn't jump on you too much, because, I did put it in symbolic terms in the book of Revelation. At least, that's where the big picture of it is.

Now, Jesus, in Matthew 24, answered this question rather plainly to the disciples, because *they* asked Him. At the beginning of the chapter they said, "Lord, what's going to happen in the future, what's going to happen to this city, to this Temple, and the end of the age, how is it going to develop?" And Jesus said that there are going to be all kinds of things in the future, in the history of the world. There will be wars, famines, earthquakes, all kinds of disasters, but *this* would not be the end. This would go on and on. However, He said that there would be persecution, religious persecution, which you've seen. Although people are not paying much attention to history, and I'm not too happy with that because that's important, to see how I have lead you in the past in order to understand how I'm going to lead you in the future. So, I wish you'd pay more attention to what went on in the middle ages and the dark ages, because *I was working then, too*. But that's another story.

To get back to your question, Jesus was saying that there would be all these things...and *the Gospel* would go to *every* nation and language and tribe...and *then* the end would come. Then He talked about what that end was.

Now before I go on, the Gospel is going forward with *greater power* and *greater speed* and *in more parts of the world* than ever before. And I hope you're noticing that. That's important.

But, the end, that Jesus said, was, *that He would come again*. He would bring angels with Him. He would come in *glory* and *power* this time. He would take up those who have put their trust in Him and learned to appreciate His love for them, *My* love for them...and He would bring them up to heaven, and the others would be destroyed by His coming. And *that* is the future of mankind.

Now, Revelation goes into more detail. And, I recognize that the symbolism is unnatural to you who have not really studied My Word, but if you'll study the rest of the Bible, especially the book of Daniel, Revelation is not that hard to understand. Even Jesus, when He was here, said, "Blessed are those who study the book of Daniel." And Revelation says, "Blessed are those who study this book." Now those are the only two books in all sixty-six books of the Bible, the only two that I have indicated there's a special blessing for studying them. And they ought to be studied together.

To Daniel, I gave very clear explanations. And if those methods of explanation that the angels gave in Daniel were applied to Revelation, you'd see *very clearly* what I have in mind, both from the details that haven't yet unfolded and the many that have, and you would see (*especially* if you look at chapters 21 and 22) that the *final* end of mankind is that mankind won't end. Because I'm going to take and create this world *anew*. It's going to be a brand new perfect world—the way I made it in the beginning. And *I'm* going to be here...and live with redeemed mankind...and *we're* going to go on *forever, together. And am I going to enjoy that.*

Boy, 9, Lexington, Kentucky:
Dear God. Is there a Santa Claus?

Ha, ha, ho, ho... That's a good one! I like that one!

There is no one person who is the Santa Claus of Christmas that children are told about. However, there are many people in the world who are loving and generous, the way Santa Claus is. Many parents are loving and generous to their children and want to give them the things that the children long for. And some of those parents have the opportunity, the wealth, to be able to give those gifts to those children. There are other parents who would love to be able to do it but don't have the money or the opportunity to do that. That doesn't mean that they are less loving or generous. And of course, parents are also wise and know that some of the things that children want are not best for them. And that's where part of the story about Santa Claus is not the best because it never tells about Santa Clause choosing something better for the child than what he or she wants.

Now, some people think that *I* am the big Santa Claus of the universe, and that if they are good, then they can ask Me for things and I will provide those things for them, and if they're not good, they won't get what they want. And that really is not a good picture; it's not a true picture because I'm more like the loving parent who *wisely* chooses to give the child only what's good for the child, but who loves the child very much and wants to be as generous as possible, and I have all of heaven and Earth with which to be abundantly generous and I do love to do that...I just love to give boys and girls good things. But I do realize that there are more important things than just giving presents to people. As good as that is and as joyous as that can be, there are more important things, and so much of the time I have to be concerned with those more important things. I'm looking forward to the day when all of that will be cared for...all of those important things will be all done and I can just lavish gifts on My children. And *you* are one of them.

Oh, I'm looking forward to the time when you can really enjoy what I have planned for you, because you haven't even begun to imagine what I have planned for you. But, that will have to wait a little while because I do have to care for these things that are so important. I hope that you will learn to trust Me with that. I hope that you will learn to see that *I do love you very much* and that you can trust Me. And that soon, very soon, these other things will be cared for, and we're going to have *the best* time, together.

In the meantime, don't worry too much about whether there is a Santa Claus or not, but appreciate your parents and the other people who love you and who are generous to you, and know that *all of that* is part of My love going to you, *even now.*

Female, Veterinarian, Rutland, Vermont:
Dear God, why are so many wonderful people, leaders, like Jesus, Gandhi, Martin Luther King, John F. Kennedy, Abraham Lincoln...why are so many great people always taken from us, and so brutally?

People were puzzled about that question when John the Baptist was beheaded. When Jesus was brought the news that John had been beheaded, He said to the people that John the Baptist was *the greatest* of all the prophets.

Now, man would generally think that *if* a person is great in My eyes that I would then protect them. That I would make sure nothing happened to that person because that person is really great in My eyes, and he's really on My side, and he's really obeying Me and doing great things for Me, and so, I'm going to protect him. But, as Isaiah said to the people, My thoughts are not your thoughts. Your ways are not My ways. My ways are higher than man's ways. So...I don't operate the same way you do, and basically it's because I see so much *more* than you do.

You see a little bit of the picture, of this world, and of the universe. And *I'm* dealing with the whole thing. I'm seeing it and dealing with it. The sins, the violence, the death, the tragedies of this world are what you're focused on. But they are part of a much bigger picture, a picture that takes in the universe.

When sin began, it wasn't in this world, it was in heaven itself. And the highest created being was the one who got involved, who tasted of selfishness, and then chose to cling to it, even when I explained that it was deadly...not only for himself but for others. And yet he would not let go. And then he *spread* that to one-third of the other angels. And the on-looking beings of other worlds were watching, and they considered the issues and had to think it through and choose how to respond. And then finally, this world was the next place where I allowed him to come and see if anyone would join him in rebellion. And when Adam and Eve decided to do that (it was their choice) this was the world where the *grand experiment*, if you want to call it that, or the *grand tragedy*, if you want to call it *that*, of selfishness could be allowed to work itself out, for the benefit of the universe.

So this world is the place for sin to happen. And therefore I'm dealing with this whole conflict of sin in the context of the grand scheme of things. And so, I have to *allow* for sin to show itself as the horrible thing it is. And part of that is that people are *hurt*...and John the Baptist is one who I could *trust* with the responsibilities of being one who is a follower of mine, and yet, undergoes tragedy.

Now, that's necessary for two reasons: one, is that other people down through the centuries since John's time, would have to give their lives for their faith in Me. And that was necessary because there were people in the world who would never learn to trust Me unless they saw someone who was willing to give their life for Me, and could see the peace that that person could have in his eyes, in his expression, in his heart—that he had peace, and a faith, and a purpose in his life…and in his death. In other words, he had something worth dying for, and others could see that and they could see they didn't have that, and they were drawn to that, and then they could come to a commitment to Me and receive the gift of eternal life. And so, many, many people were won to eternal life through the death of some. And John the Baptist going before them was then a great example that just because you have to die for your faith doesn't mean that you're forsaken of God. So that was important…but also, in this *conflict* in the universe between Me and Satan, I use the three things of *truth, freedom*, and *love*. I do not use force. Now, I have enough force to do it, I could force everybody to just obey Me, and I could force everybody to just except what I tell them. But that's not what I use. I use truth, freedom, and love. And so, because of that, I want the intelligent beings of the universe to respond to My principles and My way of doing things, My love, My character, My government; I want them to respond to those things with freedom and love and because they know it's true.

And so, I have to *reach* people with truth and with freedom. And I also *allow* a challenge. Truth is not afraid of challenge. Because truth is what it is…*it's truth*. And so it's not afraid of challenge and investigation, because the more you investigate truth, the more you see that it is true. And therefore, I allow Satan and his followers to challenge Me. And one of the challenges is that people who follow Me do so only because things are easier for them. Satan brought this up with the story of Job. He challenged Me in front of the universe, saying Job was only following Me because things were so easy for him as long as he followed Me. And I have to have people like Job who have been in difficult positions and have chosen to follow Me *even in the midst of that difficulty*...so that other people who have been in those same difficult positions can never say that the reason they never followed Me is because they were in that difficult spot.

For instance, someone may say, "*I* couldn't follow the Lord and trust Him because I got cancer. And you can't expect me to believe in a good God when I have cancer."

But I had many people who are My followers, whom I've allowed cancer to come to, and they still believe in Me and have still been able to trust Me and love Me and appreciate My goodness.

So when they say, "Well I can't trust God because my child was killed by a kidnapper or a child abuser."

And yet, I have had some of My people that I have allowed, and it's not pleasant for Me—if you can understand, I'm the One who has hurt more than anyone else and I love My children—I can hardly even say it, but, I've had to *allow* even some of the children of My followers to be struck down, whether by a child abuser or other tragedies, and *they have still* trusted Me.

So, Satan and all of his followers have not a leg to stand on, so to speak. And I'm sorry it has to be that way. I wouldn't want to allow hurt to come to anyone. Even those who don't believe in Me...*I don't want* them to hurt. But unfortunately, sin, as I told Lucifer in the beginning, *sin hurts*...and I can't stop sin without allowing some hurt first. And sin can not be blotted out completely from the universe, you can't get to a place where there's no sin and no pain and no suffering and no tragedy, until we allow some hurt...and until I can *resolve* this in a way that it will never come up again. And in a way where I only use *true freedom* and *love*.

<u>Male, 32, Mover, Fredericksburg, Virginia, U.S.A.:</u> People say, "when it's your time to go, it's your time to go." Is that true? Is there really, like, when someone gets shot, randomly...is there truth to that statement about it being their time to go?

The question is a good one because that phrase is expressed very often...and people buy into it.

When Jesus was here He said that not one sparrow falls but that the Father in heaven notices.

It's true that being infinite and divine, I am able to see everything going on at the same time, and to notice all creatures in the world, and to observe, and to *care* for each one.

And the reason Jesus said this...He went on to draw a contrast in comparison. He said, *you* are more valuable than sparrows...and God has even numbered the hairs of your head. And so, this is significant to Me, this idea, this concept that I want you to understand that *I know* every one of you. I mean, I know you more then the human mother knows her child. I know you. I know you *more* than that...I just know you intimately. I know every thing that you have ever experienced...things you don't even remember. I've watched over you from the very moment of conception; I was there, and I saw all of your potential, and saw all your future, and I have been watching you and working with you and loving you and just wanting a part in your life and in your heart, all the way through. And that's true with *every single human being*...all however many billion people there have been in the world...I have had that with every one.

Now, then, what happens at the point of death?

I know you're not thinking about the ninety year-old person who just falls asleep and is dead that evening in her bed. But you're talking about sudden deaths...the car accidents and the shootings and so on. Where was God at that point? Was He *taking* that person as some humans express it? Did I already have a *plan* for that person to die at that time? Was that his or her *time* to die? And that's what you're expressing there, clearly.

There are some problems with that way of thinking or that expression. It gives the idea that I am somewhat uncaring. It gives the idea that I have a plan, and I'm going to make My plan happen, and it doesn't matter what's going on in your life, it doesn't matter to Me what your state is...it's just that I have a plan and if I want you to die you're going to die, that's it! That's sort of more like one of these characters called the god father, who is running the show and whatever he wants he makes happen...and if somebody gets in his way he takes them out. And that, certainly, is not Me. I am not like that at all.

The life of every person is extremely important to Me...and I care about them and their feelings and their future.

And then people may get the opposite idea. Well, God isn't even around; He doesn't even care; He's not interested; He's not involved! And that, certainly, is not true at all, either. Or, God is too weak, as one writer put it. That I can't deal with everything at the same time, and I can't be involved and concerned and intervening with everything, and therefore I only intervene with the amount of things where I *can* intervene. Well, that's a misconception as well.

We must remember, that there are at stake, in this planet Earth, *extremely* important issues that are important not only for the citizens of planet Earth but they're important for *all* the citizens of *all* the universe, all the worlds throughout all the galaxies, all the millions of angels. Every thinking intelligent free being of the universe is focused on this world, and the issues that are involved here. And they are the issues of truth, and freedom, and love.

And this issue of freedom is such a tricky one.

Adam and Eve used their freedom to choose for this planet to be the planet where sin works itself out. I have to allow sin to do that. I need the universe to see how horrible it is, how it's absolutely unacceptable and must be completely destroyed when it *is* destroyed. And that those who use their freedom to buy into sin, to the point where they can no longer be delivered from the *slavery of selfishness* and sin...that those poor people will have to perish when sin is destroyed. And that's just an absolute necessity.

Anyway, that all has to be seen...and so, I can't get involved in ways in this universe that would ruin the principles of freedom. People have to be able to choose My involvement. And unfortunately that means that some have to face death at a time when they're not ready for eternity. And that's one of the great, great tragedies of sin. And the universe sees that. They're observing that. They know that there are so many more people that I would want to reach, that I would want to deliver with My love and the principles that are so dear to Me, that I could just make such a difference in their lives, and I want to, but I mustn't, and I won't violate your free choice. And unfortunately, while some people are not using their free choice to end their own lives, they are sometimes in the position where *other* people who are being careless use their freedom in a way that causes the death of an innocent person, shall we say. And that's highly tragic. It's My great heartache.

When Jesus was here and He was journeying to Jerusalem, and it was Palm Sunday, and the spirits of the people were so excited, they thought Jesus was going into the city to take the throne, and they put the palms down on the road, and they put their garments and their coats and carpets on the roadway for Jesus to go on...and they were so excited—but then they stopped because they noticed something. They saw Jesus weeping. He had stopped on the brow of the hill and He was looking over the city of Jerusalem, and He began to weep. Not just a quiet, soft weeping, but a *heaving* kind of weeping that a parent would weep when he was at the funeral of his child. And as Jesus was weeping the people couldn't understand it. But the reason was that He had looked over a city that was *refusing* what He had to offer. And He said to all of Jerusalem, "How I long to gather you together like a hen gathers her chicks, and I wanted to help you, I wanted to deliver you, I wanted to protect you, I wanted to be your Savior...but you won't let Me."

And Jesus knew they were going to destruction, and soon the armies of Rome would come and surround the city and lay siege, and there would be such a long, terrible experience that people would be even killing their own children because of starvation within the city, and people would be taken, and thousands upon thousands were crucified all around on the hillsides around Jerusalem, and it was a horrible tragedy. But not only that, He saw all the other people of this planet that He wouldn't be able to save. And He wept, fully, with convulsions of weeping. And that wasn't just Him, that was Me, too, and the Holy Spirit.

It's been hard watching the numbers of people *lost* in this world. That's been hard. And of everyone in the universe, We are the Ones who most want this whole thing to end. But We won't end it until it can be ended completely...and forever. That's when We'll do it. And We will make sure that it will never rise up again. You can trust Us for that.

As to the aspect of your question regarding *timing*, and that expression that people use, "it was his time to go," there are situations where I am invited to intervene in people's lives, and I do work so that a person actually does meet their death at what I see is the best time for them to do so.

Take for an example David Livingston who was found dead kneeling by his bed. He had died during his prayer time while talking to Me that evening, just before going to bed. That was a great time for him to die...and I was honoring someone there who had honored Me in such a great way in his life of unselfish love.

And then there are people who want Me to guide and direct in their lives, so I allow their deaths to take place. And sometimes it seems like a premature death, but, I know what would lie ahead for that person, because I not only know the future, the real future as it will unfold, but I also know *all possible futures*, and so I know what heartache, or mistakes, or problems that person would face, or someone else would face *because of them* if they continued to live, and so, sometimes I allow the person to meet death at a time where they wouldn't choose...but if they're allowing Me to fully reign in their lives, then certainly I can work that out in a way that doesn't detract from their freedom. So, I'm willing to do that.

Again, I want to do as much for a person as they will let Me. And if a person trusts Me completely, and lets Me work, not only through their life, but even through the circumstances of their death...I will do that. And one day when they are raised back to life, I'm looking forward to the opportunity of sharing with that person *why* they meet death at the time when they did. I know that as they hear My explanation and review the circumstances, (being able to see the other side of the loom), they will thank Me. They will thank Me for what I have done, and We will rejoice together at what was accomplished through My plans.

Male, 52, Contractor, Cedar Rapids, Iowa:

Dear God,

What's going on with all of these Alien sightings and so forth? Are there Aliens? Is there life on other planets? Have they visited Earth? Have they abducted people? And are those signs in the wheat fields across the world – have the signs been made from the Aliens or are they man-made?

People who study the heavens—the astronomers and such—have noticed that My creation is vast. I know, to you, the world seems very large much of the time, but it's very small compared to the galaxy that you are traveling in, and the groupings of galaxies that are all around you. The billions and billions of stars I designed *not* to be empty. I want a large family. I haven't said too much about this in the Bible, because, again, too much information can be confusing. There are so many other important issues to be dealt with during your short life on Earth that I don't want you to get side-tracked or distracted from those important issues.

However, I've indicated a little bit in the scriptures. One of the clearest indications is in the Book of Job, the first two chapters. It says there that the Sons of God came together in the courtroom of heaven, the throne of heaven, and they presented themselves before Me. And it mentions that Satan came there, and there was discussion, and I asked Satan where was he from. He said he was from Earth. Now, of course, *I knew* where Satan was from, because I know everything. But it was just like when I asked Adam, when Adam had sinned, "Adam, where are you?" I called out to him…and then he presented himself. Now I knew where Adam was, but I was giving *him* the opportunity to respond in the way that he chose. Again, those issues of freedom are very important to Me.

So I asked Lucifer, "Where are you going?" And he was bragging, saying, "I'm going up and down *in* the Earth, and I'm going to and fro, I can do whatever I want down on planet Earth, because, planet Earth belongs to me. That is my domain and everybody there is on my side."

And then I brought up to Satan, "Well, what about Job, he's not on your side?"

Without going further into the story, I want you to recognize that Satan was there representing this Earth. Now, I didn't intend for Satan to be the representative of this Earth...Adam was supposed to be the representative of this Earth. In fact, the word *Adam*, means *mankind*. It doesn't mean just man. It means mankind. Adam was created to be the father of the human race and to represent all of humanity at the courtroom of heaven. He was to be like the representative of the human race in the courtroom or in the *congress* of heaven.

Again, the issues of freedom—remember, I want a free universe where the beings are represented and issues of freedom are constantly being understood and enjoyed.

So, these other Sons of God that came to My court were also representatives from worlds across the universe, and they were all assembled before Me. And here, Satan, was smugly challenging My authority, not only My authority, but, more to the point, My principles of government and My methods of attaining allegiance from My creatures. So, definitely I have intelligent creatures throughout the universe. Some of them you know as angels. But there are others who inhabit various parts of the universe, various planets and all.

Now, you asked the question, "What about these visits from space ships and alien creatures and abductions, and all of that?"

It's important for Me to solve this problem of sin. Rebellion in a family is very destructive. And the rebellion that's taken place in the heavenly family with Satan, and now with this planet Earth, has been very painful. Not only to human beings, but to Me, and to the angels…and even to onlooking planets, because it's really the focal point of the universe now—to see how this problem of sin is going to work itself out, and how the principles of selfishness, *how they* work themselves out. Because again, My principle is so important, so dear to Me, because I know it's the only thing that can lead to true fulfillment, true happiness, true freedom, and true love—it *is* true love. It's unselfish love. That principle is absolutely necessary. And when Satan rebelled against that, and said, no, he could do it another way; Well now, I've given him the opportunity to do that. And the universe is looking on and I am *not allowing* interaction between the rest of the universe and this world, except as there are certain agreed upon opportunities for My intervention in this world. And, as is indicated there by that story with Job, *there is* interaction. There's allowance for Satan to accomplish certain things. There is also allowance for *Me* to accomplish certain things. That's where prayer comes in, because when people *freely ask* for intervention, that's when I can come in and intervene...and do *more* than when there's not a free request for My involvement. That's why Jesus said when people pray there's a response...when two or three people pray, there's a *greater* response. Because again, I want to preserve the issues of freedom. That's got to be preserved. At all cost, really. Because, without it, there is no real love, and therefore, no real happiness.

So, I'm not allowing interaction from other worlds on this planet...aside from the involvement of the angels. And you can discover more about their interactions by reading the scriptures.

However, your question then, of course, would be, well then where are these aliens coming from?

Remember that Lucifer, who became Satan, was the most powerful angel. He had the most talent, the most gifts, the most power of any...the most intelligence of any. He was the leader. And he *still* has those powers...and in the Bible I've indicated that he has the ability to present himself even as an angel of light. In other words, he can take various forms and appear to be what he wants to appear to be. He could appear to be an alien, for instance. He can also accomplish amazing things, such as these symbols in the wheat fields. He and the other angels with him have the power to take these various life forms, if you want to call them that, or appearances, and seek to deceive human beings by what he's doing.

Jesus talked about how a lot of deception would take place in the end time...and the Book of Revelation says, in chapter 13, especially, that in the end time Satan will be working with greater power to do *wonders* and *miracles*. Jesus said that Satan would perform so many miracles that it would almost deceive even My special chosen people, the ones who really know Me and love Me. Even for them, it would be a challenge to sort out what's real and what's not real.

And so, I do want you to be very careful not to be taken in just because something is very dramatic and very real and very *supernatural*. That doesn't mean it's from God; it doesn't mean it's from another planet. Satan has the ability to disguise himself and to masquerade in all different forms. And this is one of the things that appeals to human beings today, because it's talking about space journey and interacting with other worlds, and it really fits into science fiction entertainment and all of that. So, people are really captivated by it, it's very fascinating to them. But please don't let this distract you from the central issues, which concern problems of sin, rebellion, selfishness...versus to know Me, to trust Me, to learn My ways of unselfishness, and true love, true freedom…those are so important…don't let this detract you.

Male, 59, Banker, Stockholm, Sweden:
God,
Why is the world, especially America…why is it in financial turmoil, moral turmoil, and why has it become, under the present administration, a war-monger nation?

The answer to your question goes back to the very beginning of the Bible, Genesis, chapter 3, where mankind, in Adam and Eve, chose selfishness, the ways of Satan. And that became part of man's nature.

In Psalm 51, David said that he was born in sin and shaped in iniquity.

So, man *is* by nature rebellious, sinful, and selfish. He wants to be independent and do his own thing. And so, the nature of man has not changed. It reveals itself in different ways in different times and in different cultures. During the Middle Ages, there was a lot of superstition, and people were afraid. The church leaders, the so-called church leaders, and other people in power took advantage of that…and built on it, and tried to keep knowledge from the people. And so, their selfishness came out with that kind of *grasping* for power.

The Bible says that the love of money is the root of all evil, so, financial problems come because of people grasping for money. And right now in the western world there's such an emphasis on the bottom line—not service, not helping others, not making a contribution to society—but, *What is in it for me*? What are *we going to make* from this project or from this merger? And that has led to financial trouble. Because, what goes around comes around—there's so much truth in that. Jesus said it a different way, "That measure with which you measure unto others, the same will be measured unto you."

So, if the western capitalist world gets so focused on what is in it for themselves, then that's going to come around and have it's negative influence on them later. And that later is now. That's happened.

The moral issues, of course, *also* relate to that sinful nature of man. And because the western world, and now so much of the world, really, has become better off than it was before, and there's a lot of prosperity around that allows people more time and money to get themselves into trouble. And so, the immorality has increased.

The question about being warmongers. Well, again, the grasping...

The United States started out very good in many ways. Not perfect, but, *just good* in many ways. Because of their emphasis on two things, which relate to the issues of freedom that are so important to Me. One was that this would be a nation in which there would be a new kind of freedom for the citizens, because the *land* would be governed by the people. And Lincoln said so well, "A government of the people, by the people, and for the people." So the people had the freedom to govern themselves. And the *other* freedom, which is even more important to Me, is the freedom of people to worship according to their own conscience. And so this was a whole new government. The first major country to have this kind of freedom. So I was anxious to bless this country, and I have, over many years. (And the people have responded in that this has been a land that has been very *giving.*) Over the decades, and now centuries, there have gone out from the United States missionaries, and doctors, and all kinds of religious and humanitarian efforts to bring healing and help and the gospel to the world. And it's been wonderful. I've just enjoyed blessing this so much.

In recent years, unfortunately, the love of money and the love of ease have taken over more and more and more. And while there is still much giving, it's not nearly what it could be and what it should be. So, the moral depravity has been allowed to increase. And it's very sad, what's happening there. Actually, I know that it's going to get worse; it's not going to get better. I've even indicated this in Revelation, chapter 13. But the United States finds itself in a difficult situation because it's the major leading power in the world now and it does have a responsibility to help freedom be *preserved* as much as possible in other parts of the world, and to use it's influence and power to accomplish that. And to protect, not only the United States itself, but its allies and other freedom-loving nations around the world, from harm by those who are basically, to the greatest degree, ready to follow Satan's ways rather than Mine. And so while the United States isn't perfect, there are human forces in the world who are so closely aligned with Satan's kingdom that there is some interaction needed, some intervention by the United States, or other nations that would join with the United States, in seeking to preserve freedom and protection for the other inhabitants of the world.

So, I don't want to say that the United States is a war-mongering nation. While I recognize there are motivations of selfishness involved, there are *also* motivations of preserving freedom and life. And I hope that the peoples of other countries will *not be blinded* by the selfishness they see, so that they cannot see the good humanitarian efforts and motives of many of the American people. And I hope that they won't be turned off by the gospel that these good American people are trying to present to the world. I want to use whoever—whether they're American or Chinese or African or whatever...I want to use anyone who knows Me well and who wants to share My principles of freedom and unselfish love...I'm ready to use them. And I hope that others can look beyond their national affiliations and listen to the message itself so that they can learn to know Me and to trust Me.

Female, 17, Providence, Rhode Island:
Dear God, will there ever be a female President of the United States?

Well, you're asking Me to reveal the future to you. Which I have been willing to do, but, I am selective in what aspects of the future that I reveal. Now, you may misinterpret that, as some have. You may think that I'm trying to be controlling by only letting them know a little bit and holding the rest for Myself. And, Satan likes to build that up and try to make it look like the thing I'm interested in is to keep My position as the One ruler of the universe, and nobody else is allowed to come anywhere *near* having any power and authority that I have. And, boy, that's not it at all. However, one who *has* power and authority has a great responsibility to use that power and authority *wisely*. In fact, that's why I was *so* pleased when I offered *anything* to Solomon, who was a brand new young king, and the one thing he asked for was *wisdom* to use his authority and the kingdom in a good way to rule the people wisely. What a tremendous thing. But that's tremendous in how it reflects My attitude. I want to use My power and authority wisely, only in ways that build *up* My creatures, My sons and daughters. I want them to have everything that's good. I recognize that not everything is good at any given time. Not everything is helpful, *including* knowledge of the future. And so, I hold it back because I recognize that it can *hurt*.

I don't want you to hurt. I don't want to spoil things. Some things are just better not shared. There are things that are good to share about the future and *those* I have revealed. You already have them available in the Bible, especially in the books of Daniel and Revelation. But other books of the Bible refer to the future. And the main event of the future, or focus of what I've revealed about the future, is that of the Second Coming of Jesus, and the things that surround it. And really, if you have the hope of the assurance of the Second Coming of Jesus, and that you are ready today and day by day for that great event, then whether or not there is a female president or whether or not that communism in China will ever fall or Islam will cause more wars…those things are not nearly as important. The event of Christ's Second Coming is *supremely* important. Because that's going to end all of the nations and the wars and the tragedies and the natural disasters; all of that will come to an end, because Jesus will then set up My kingdom and His kingdom, which will be eternal, and all the others will pass away.

So, I don't want to distract you by revealing these other things. In the scriptures, there's really a lot there…in the books of Daniel and Revelation, but Revelation focuses more on the time you're living in, right up to the Second Coming of Jesus. And it talks about some *really* interesting events. If you want to know about the United States, look at Revelation 13, especially the second half. I know it's a little tricky and hard for you to understand, but if you read that and then go back to Daniel, chapters 2, 7, and 8, and then come back to Revelation 13, I think you'll start to see the pieces, and the Holy Spirit will help you. And you can find others who can help you with that, too, if you'll search. But, the scripture is intended to interpret itself. Don't rely on man's interpretations, go back to the Bible and let the Bible explain itself, and that's where Daniel will help you, because the angel explained to Daniel what the symbols meant. Then follow that pattern. Take the pattern that the angel gave in Daniel and apply it to Revelation. You'll be amazed by how much you can understand about what it says there—the *importance* of the events that are going to unfold *in* the United States before Jesus returns. And I want you to know about it because I want you to be ready. You can steer clear of Satan's work and his deceptions that will, unfortunately, sway so many, so much of the population. If you'll follow My Word, you can be ready. The Holy Spirit will help you. You can be ready to *know* the truth and to *stand* for the truth, and be ready for Jesus to return. And I sure want you to be among those. I'm looking forward to it. I'm going to do everything I can to help you. I can be successful, if you will trust Me. I am successful every time with everyone who trusts Me. And you will be ready. You will come home, and, We've got a lot of good stuff planned to do together in eternity. So don't miss it.

Male, 54, Screen Writer, Cleveland, Ohio:
Dear God,
I just wanted to thank you. I smoked for over forty years. I came down with throat cancer. I had some serious operations, but I've turned it around. I quit drinking and smoking. I haven't talked to You since I was a little boy, but I have been talking to You lately and communicating with You and I attribute my better health to those conversations. I want to thank You. No question—just thanks.

You don't realize how utterly valuable to Me were those times when you turned to Me. I was just waiting for you to share, and I have rejoiced every time when you opened up your heart to Me and came to Me, whether it was with a problem such as your health or whether it was with some joy...just sharing whatever life brought to you...and I just cherish those times. And now, I appreciate your thanks.

When Jesus was on Earth and He healed ten lepers at one time, only one returned to thank Him, but that one was a tremendous encouragement to Christ in His ministry, who oftentimes was discouraged because so few responded. And so today, you are that one that brings joy to My heart. Thank *you*.

Female, 23, Billings, Montana:
Dear God. We hear about how old dinosaur bones found are sometimes millions of years old. And, other things discovered are hundreds of thousands of years old. My question — how old is the planet Earth?

If you could, in your imagination, join Me in going back in time to the Garden of Eden, that first week when I created all things, as I've described there in Genesis 1 and 2. And you watch various things appear as I speak them into existence. And then you watch as I create Adam. Now, you look at Adam…how old is he? I should say, how old does he *appear*? Twenty? Twenty-five? Thirty? And yet, how old is he? A few minutes? A human being who is only a few minutes old should weigh about six pounds and be about twenty inches long, right? And that's your experience, anyway. But, if you looked at Adam and Eve, they would not be six pounds and twenty inches long. They would appear to be full-grown adults. Years, really decades, old. And if you went over and looked at a tree—suppose you cut down a tree there in the Garden of Eden, when I had just created it a couple of days before—how many rings would it have? And would it appear years old? And the rocks—if you looked at the rocks, rocks take a long time to form in the world today. So, everything that you look at would *appear* to be very old. Even the stars in the sky, stars are a hundred thousand light-years away. And so the light…*they say* the light has taken that long to reach Earth, therefore, the stars must be a hundred thousand years old. But, you forget, suppose I created the stars *and* all the light between the stars and Earth. Then, maybe something that appears to be old, isn't so old.

If you read through the Bible and put together

all the stories, you'll find that the world is several thousand years old. But not hundreds of thousands of years...or millions—although it appears to be. But what are you going to trust, your limited observations, or what I have told you? I think I'll leave it at that.

Female, 42, Kona, Hawaii:
Dear God,
I put my faith and trust in You regarding Your will for me...but, could You please show me Your presence on a daily basis?

You use the phrase, "on a daily basis." This indicates to Me that you *have* felt My presence or sensed My presence *at times* just not on a daily basis. And that's more than a lot of people can say of their whole lifetimes. They don't sense My presence or My involvement in their lives through most of their lives which is something very sad to Me. But, let Me not be detracted with others and their experiences, let Me focus on you and your question.

I am so pleased that you *want* to sense My presence. That's such a tremendous response to what I have been trying to do to appeal to you...to win your trust. So many are afraid of Me and they run from My presence. They're just afraid of Me. They're afraid of what I will do. Or what I will demand. And it just delights Me that I sense that you are one who is learning to trust Me more and to know that

I am here to help you, not to hurt you—never to hurt. As a loving parent, I just long to envelope you in My arms and provide that sense of My presence for you. And, indeed, I do offer and provide for you a sense of My presence each day in many ways.

But, many times, you, like the rest of humanity, have a life to live in this world of so many demands and needs and distractions. It's hard for you, I know, and I'm sympathetic to the difficulty of it—for you to slow down and to observe the things that I am sending your way.

It does help for you to take the time to open your heart to Me in prayer...and then be quiet, and listen for Me to respond to you and impress our heart with the message of My love and truth. But another *big* help is for you to praise Me. Now, I say that, not because I am an egotistical dictator of the universe who loves to just hear My name upheld and praised. Don't get the wrong picture. But I want to encourage you to praise Me because the universe runs on this great principle of Mine—unselfish love. And when you praise Me, it's an aspect of loving someone else. You'll be loving Me and expressing that love in praise to Me.

In human terms, when a man and a woman fall in love and they're in that enthusiasm of romantic love, they express that. They *tell* each other how wonderful they see that other one. And so, when you express wonderful things about Me that you observe, it's a way of opening your heart to love.

Remember, the scripture says that God is love. I *am* love. You are then opening you heart to Me—to My presence. And so the more you praise Me, the more *often* you praise Me, the more you will have a sense of My presence with you. When you are taking time for prayer, take *more* of that time for praise than you do for requests...either for yourself or for others. Now, don't leave those things out altogether because that's an important part, too, of our relationship—for you to be able to share with Me how you are feeling and what your needs are and how I can be involved in your life. That's still great. But do take time to look for *new things* to praise Me for.

When you see a beautiful sunset or sunrise, praise Me for My creativity and for My power to create such vast things. When you look into a microscope and see the tiny things of creation that still have order and precision, you can praise Me for My abilities to create such an intelligent and well designed universe. When you see human beings acting in loving and unselfish ways as they're inspired by My truth and love, you can praise Me for the wonder of what My love can accomplish.

So, look for all kinds of things and try to be very open to seeing more of the different facets of My abilities and My character. As you do that, you will sense more of My presence. You can do that all through the day and in all different situations. As you make that a habit, you will sense more and more of My presence with you.

Female, 44, Sheriff, Simi Valley, CA, USA:
God... Why wasn't I made a man? Because being a male in this society is better, I feel. They have more control, more benefits, are treated better, have more advantages. Because of the job that I'm in, I'm in a man's world.

What your question is really all about is, *why is there inequality and injustice in the world*? Because if men and woman were truly equal and if there was real justice and fairness in the world, men and woman would be treated equally, at least in the sense that if they were making equal contributions they would be reimbursed with equal compensation, and each person would be appreciated for what they could contribute whether they were of a certain sex or some other characteristic that separates people.

So the question really goes back to why is there injustice. Because the short person asks, "Why wasn't I created tall?" And the tall person asks, "Why wasn't I created average?" The poor person asks, "Why wasn't I created rich?" The person born in Africa asks, "Why wasn't I born in the United States or some other wealthy country?" And we could go on and on. All of it relates to the problem that this world is a place where there's injustice and there is tragedy and heartache, there is inhumanity of man to man...or maybe I should say, *person to person.* I don't want to be insensitive, and I'm not insensitive. Because I...I hurt for you, with you, and with all these others that we have mentioned. I *don't want* there to be injustice in the world. I don't want there to be heartache and inequality. That's not the real meaning of the world.

In the beginning, the world was *very good.* In fact, it was perfect. A perfect place. And when I made Eve from Adam, I didn't take a piece of bone out of his foot, symbolizing that he was completely above her. I took the bone from the *side* of his body to show that she was to be an equal—someone to be cherished and to walk together with. But, sin came in, and with it came the heartache, the inequality, the injustice, the tragedy, and the death. And with every heart that hurts, I hurt...and, I'm sorry that you have to face this. However, do look on the positive things. It's not easy, I know. I don't mean for it to sound as if it's easy, but you do have opportunities that others have not had. You do live in a society where there *are* freedoms and benefits that other societies in the past or in other places have not had and do not have.

There is a special talent...no, not talent, it's really a *gift* of being content with whatever you have, with whatever your situation is. It's not a gift that you can give yourself, but it is a gift that I can give you. The Apostle Paul talked about it...he said that he *learned* to be content, whether he was prosperous or whether he was poor, whether he was strong or weak, free or in jail. And, *it showed* because he could sing even when he was chained to a prison cell. And others have had it, too.

The key is to know Me and trust Me. And as you do that, you will realize that I am able to work *all things* together for good to those who love Me and are called according to My purpose, those who put themselves in My hands for Me to *work out* what I can, what I want to. And when you have that sense, then a *peace* comes that you can't have any other way. And the peace provides the contentment. And then, because you are content, you can be grateful for what you have. You can rejoice. There is really no better way to live. I'll teach you...if you want.

Female, 16, Tashkent, Uzbekistan:
Dear God. Why don't men give birth?

Ha, ha, ha... That's definitely a question from a female. Men don't have any wonder about that.

Let's see...why don't men give birth?

When the Three of Us in the Godhead decided to create the planet Earth, We planned it to be the first world where there would be creatures who were created with the ability to have a major part in creation, especially in creating someone in their own image. We had to make some decisions about the designs of the creatures, of course, as We were creating this world with this particular aspect to it—with the attention of the angels and other intelligent creatures from other parts of the universe who would now be able to understand a little bit more about Us, the Godhead.

We, from the beginning of creating intelligent beings, recognized that one of the great challenges that We would have as infinite creators, was to have the finite creatures understand Us, and We would need to *speak their language* in order to communicate with them. So, We realized that it would be a step-by-step process. We'd be able to reveal a little bit about what We are like, then a little more, and a little bit more, and so on. And a part of this process was that the three of Us would take different roles. I, the Father, took the role of revealing the great glory, majesty, and power of God as the ruler of the universe. So that as the creatures learned about Me, they were learning those aspects of divinity. But then, the One referred to as the Son, or Jesus, or previously as Michael, He took the role of putting aside the glory of power in order to come to the level of the creatures. As Michael, the Archangel, He became first an angel so that the beings of heaven would know Him on their level and see His character demonstrated in terms with which they were familiar. Later on, He became Jesus Christ on Earth, and as a human being helped the human race understand the true character qualities of divinity, on their own level, the things with which they're familiar. And the Holy Spirit took the role of being the One who could work right *in the minds* and *hearts* of the individual creatures all at the same time, by giving them inspired understandings of the evidence before them, whether in the Bible, or in creation, or in other things. The human beings would be able, *with His help*, to put together all the evidence and understand about the three of Us better.

So We decided We would need to take those three roles in order for the intelligent creatures to look at each of those three aspects and be able to combine that picture so that they could understand that each of Us has *all three* aspects, or qualities…and that would be helpful. So, when We created this world, We wanted to take the step of helping intelligent creatures to understand something about Our creative power. And how it was out of Our love, the aspect of unselfish love, that We wanted to create creatures in Our image, whom We could love and who could love Us…and who could share in the joy of life and love. And so, when We designed mankind, humanity, so that they would be able to have a major involvement in creating someone in their own image, We decided to give them different roles…so that the male would be one who would contribute the sperm that would then be combined with the egg in the woman, and then she would have the womb and house the developing fetus, and then give birth. So they would have different roles to play. Designing the male to have one role and the female to have another, We desired to help the intelligent creatures of the universe understand that in the Godhead there are different roles that We've taken. It doesn't mean that one is greater than the other or less than the other…but it's just different, different roles. But, together We're one, We're in harmony, and We can do marvelous things in Our creation.

So, man is different from woman. They have different roles, but together they are one and thereby have incredible abilities to *create*. If We were to give man also the role of pregnancy in birth, just as the woman has, then there wouldn't be a difference, and We would lose that opportunity to share that point of truth about Us, Ourselves…and that was valuable, We didn't want to lose that, so We made mankind with those differences.

Now, why it had to be the female and not the male…well, it didn't really *have to be*, but somebody had to have one, and one the other. Just like among Us in the trinity or in the Godhead, One of Us would have to be on the throne, another One would have to be on the level with the creatures, another One would have to be the unseen comforter, and We just came to an agreement in making Our choices. We'd all be willing to do the work of the other, and able to, but, somebody had to do something, so, We chose and We did. And I know that the women who are hearing this answer may feel that that's not fair that the woman has to go through all the agony and the pain and the man doesn't and only gets the pleasure part. But, that's not really true. If you're looking at just the birth, yes, it's painful and traumatic, and the pregnancy, too, that's not always pleasant—however, there's a joy that a woman has with their child that a man isn't part of because he doesn't get to do the part that she does.

And so, that's just the way it is. Just like, as the Father, I'm on the throne, somewhat detached from My creation, where as Jesus got to be right there and could live and interact with and be so close to humanity. I didn't get to do that. Do we want to say that's not fair? I don't look at it that way, because, first of all, I see the joy that Jesus experienced and I rejoiced that *He* could have such joy. And when He hurt, I hurt—when He was on the Cross.

So, there's got to be some differences. But, let's not let those differences rob us of the *joy* that comes with them, that we can get in seeing the good that's coming to the other.

Male, 21, U.S. Army, 82nd Airborne, Fort Bragg, NC:
Dear God,
I believe that soon I will be deployed to the Middle East. How do I go off to war and fight and possibly kill for our country…how do I do that in Your eyes?

One human said, "War is hell." And *I* would certainly say that war *comes* from hell. It's not what *I* want for humanity. Though, sometimes, there have arisen individuals, or groups of people, who have so aligned themselves with evil, and who have been so bent on causing destruction, trying to take over other people, dominating ruthlessly or trying to wipe out the truth about Myself in the world, that war has been a necessity. If you've read My Word, you have seen that there are times when I directed David, for example, to make war against other people. And David destroyed them, completely. So, at times, there's been no other way to handle situations.

Now, the challenge you're facing is that your *country* not I, is asking you to go to war. If *I* asked you to go to war the way I did to the Israelites, by My direct command, you would have an easier time recognizing what your duty truly is.

You did ask, "How would it be in My eyes?" Now when your country asks you to go to war, then you're put into a hard spot. Because, as the apostles said when they were told that they *must not* continue preaching in the name of Jesus, they determined that they must obey God rather than man. Other times, they recognized that it was their duty to obey the government as much as possible. But when they saw that the government laws forbade them doing the very thing I commanded them to do, they put My commands above the commands of their national leaders. So that's the challenge that you have. Are My commands more important to you than the commands of your national leaders?

Jesus talked about having enemies, but He said to pray for your enemies, pray for those who would abuse you or persecute you, turn the other cheek when you're hit on the one. And, today, I have followers in all different countries of the world. So, if someone in the United States is a follower of Mine and goes into the army and is fighting...and someone who is My follower in a different country—the "other country"—and he is in his respective army, fighting…then these two are shooting at each other, and they're *both* followers of Mine. For instance, many Americans think that Iraq is made up of only Muslims. But indeed, there are Christians, as well, living in Iraq.

So, the war doesn't have anything to do with whether someone is *opposed* to truth and righteousness, evil or good. They may just have a different opinion on what is a correct form of government. Or what is correct boundaries or territories, or what is the correct methods of trade or something of that nature—human problems and human difficulties and perspectives. They haven't even really asked Me…the government leaders haven't even asked for what *I* would want or what I see as the solution that could be provided.

So, I just challenge you to pick up My Word and read the principles that I made more plain in the New Testament than the Old, more plain in the teachings of Jesus than other places. And then…ask Me to help you sort it all out. The Holy Spirit stands ready to do that very thing. And, you can understand what your duty is.

And the other part of the question is, "Well, I'm *already* a soldier, and I can't decide now whether I'm going to be a soldier or not. A soldier has to go and fight. How can I do that?"

Well, the thing is…and let Me start this way…you may, in your study of the Bible and your asking for My conviction as to what's right and wrong for you, you may come to the conclusion that you, indeed, cannot go into battle and kill the enemy. Yet you are a soldier who's expected to do that. Well, the question needs to ring in your ears—is it right, is it better to obey God or to obey man? And in other times and in other places people have had to take a stand for Me above their officers, their governments, their country. It's not been easy, but they have taken that stand. And if you decide to do that, I will be with you. I'm not saying I'm going to take away the problem, but I will be with you *in* facing the problem. And at the right time and in the right way, I will honor you. I will honor you.

Male, 52, Little Rock, Arkansas:
Dear God,
Could you please comment on what You see when You look at the debate that we're having here on Earth about the separation of Church and State? Prayers in public schools and so forth?

Like most things that human beings deal with, this idea, this issue of separation of church and state has become multifaceted. You have, in the United States, people from many different backgrounds, different experiences, different concerns, different perspectives, and when they look at any issue, the issue becomes multifaceted because of all these different perspectives coming to bear upon it. And so this is true with *this* issue. People perceive this issue in many different ways and with different emphases. So, when one person thinks of separation of church and state, they're thinking that this is a good thing, because it keeps the government from controlling religion or religion from controlling the government. This, indeed, was the intention of so many of the people who first came to the United States from Europe. They were getting away from a society in which religion and government were so closely connected that people were being persecuted based on religious convictions. They wanted government to be separate from religion so that religious leaders neither influenced the government nor tried to control others; conversely, the government could not control religion, any religion, or stop people from worshipping in certain ways.

Other people look at the separation of church and state as a bad thing. They think this is bad because American society is getting less religious. They think that it's because the government enforced this separation and not only have they enforced it, the government's gone beyond the original intention. While they're willing to accept that government shouldn't control religion, they're not willing to accept that religion should stay out of government issues altogether. And, indeed, some of that perspective is correct. Because you can't have a society where religion *is* entirely separated from the policies and laws of the government in that country, because government has to deal with laws regarding behavior. Behavior is ethical, and ethics are certainly tied to religious ideas. So the debate goes back and forth.

Of course, the person who doesn't want any religion in *his* life at all is happy to have religion completely out of government and public schools, and not tied to society in general or the public institutions. On the other hand, the person who is religious wants religion to impact *his* society, and to protect his set of values.

Now, you're asking Me, though, for My perspective.

As I've indicated in the great flow of thought in the Bible—the flow of this great story of the struggle between Myself and Satan that began before this world was created, but has continued on. This world *has* become the great center stage of the universe where all can behold the differences between Satan's ways and My ways. One of the central issues is the issue of freedom. That's *the* central issue. Freedom. Satan claims that I don't allow freedom. And I have tried to make it very clear that not only do I allow freedom but I *value* it, I treasure it, so much so that in Christ I was willing to give *everything* to preserve freedom. So I do not force anyone—to love Me, to worship Me, to serve Me. In fact, in the first chapter in Isaiah, I have expressed so clearly that *I can't stand it* when people feel that forced obedience is what I want, that worship that just goes through the motions is acceptable to Me—it's not at all. I only want worship that is *thoughtful* and *meaningful*, and freely offered *to* Me. That's the only kind that's *acceptable* to Me. I love the idea of a free society where people are truly free to worship Me as they are convicted and as they chose. And this is one of the great reasons why I have poured out blessings on the United States of America—because it was really the first society where people were allowed to worship Me as they choose, according to the dictates of their conscience. I am glad that there have always been enough people in the United States to preserve that freedom…and I want that to continue. This is why in the United States—while there has been much selfishness and pride and things of that nature that the rest of the world has seen, and that's certainly not something that has My approval or that represents Me correctly—at the same time there *has* been much *un*selfishness and generosity, compassion, cherishing of life, standing up for the underdog, and those kind of things that *do* represent My character well. There has been *a lot* of that in the United States. Because, *people have been allowed the freedom to worship as they choose.* And it's led to the development of thought and creativity, and just a lot of things that have been a great blessing, not only within the borders of America, but have gone throughout the world and have blessed all mankind. There have been more missionaries and doctors and disaster relief workers that have gone out from the United States than from anywhere else in the world. And so much of it is dependent upon freedom of people to worship.

I'm glad that there has been this separation where the government can't control religion and religion can't control government—that's the good thing. Now, any good thing taken to an extreme becomes a bad thing. And that's where you're getting into trouble, because on both sides there are people who want to take things to an extreme. There are people who want to make it so that *never* in a government institution or public school or any public setting can any reference to Me be acceptable. That becomes a violation of freedom, because they're not letting people have any freedom to express their regard for divinity or a creator. Then there are the people at the other extreme who want to be able to push for the elections of those who will represent *their* particular religious thoughts and convictions in order to make laws that will try to *enforce* their convictions on others.

And so there has to be this debate. If there were no debate on this issue, *that* would be a bad thing, because it would indicate that no one is thinking, no one is thinking for one's self, no one is regarding as valuable one's own perspectives, one's own ideas. So they're not sharing them with anybody...and that would be a bad thing. I'm *glad* that people are thinking these things through, struggling with them, and trying to work them through *with others*. Now, it's not a good thing if you just take your own ideas and you say, well *I'm not going to believe anything else, I'm not going to listen to anybody else, this is the way it is.*

I want you to be able to hold your convictions strongly, *but listen to others.* Try to see things from their perspective, so that you can grow. And you can respect the intelligence and the freedom of other people. *That's* when you'll become a lot like Me. Because, remember, freedom of My intelligent creatures is a *treasure* to Me. So treasure that for others. That would be great.

Now, as to prayer in the public schools...nobody is taking prayer out of the public schools. *I'm* hearing prayers from public schools everyday...by the thousands...by the millions. There are young people across the United States who, everyday, go into the classrooms, and before they take a test or other situations, they stop and silently lift up a prayer for My help, My guidance. And *no one* can stop them. No one. No one has.

So you moms and dads and pastors who are concerned about prayer in the public school...just teach your young people *to pray.* Themselves. Privately. No one can stop it. Don't feel, though, that you have to have *every*body participating in a group prayer. That's not necessary. It is so easy for them to become just habit. I really treasure those young people who, on their own, lift their hearts up to Me. And I hear every word. And I answer those prayers. Every one. And I know they are going to continue. And that delights Me.

Male, 19, Grocery Bagboy, Putnam, Connecticut:
Hello God. Paper or plastic?

Ha, ha, ha. Oh, boy. Ha, ha, ha.

Neither. I'll just put them in My pockets. I have *really big* pockets.

Female, 28, Warsaw, Poland:
Question – In different times in the Bible, or in different sermons or stories, we hear about Jesus one time and then about God another time, but sometimes it seems like they're talking about the same person. Are Jesus and God separate beings? Or are they just different names for the same one being? And at the time of the Second Coming, will Jesus appear or will God appear? Or both?

The three members of the Godhead—Father, Son, and Holy Spirit—are three distinct persons who share a special oneness. At the baptism of Jesus are seen three Persons who are united in Our interest in, commitment to, and involvement in the plan of salvation for mankind. We are identical in character, powers, eternal being, essence, and goals. Unselfish love is at the core of our beings.

Out of love towards Our intelligent creatures We decided to take different roles in order to help them understand the different aspects of divinity. I, the Father, took the role of the Ruler of the universe. I portray the infinite power, glory, majesty and authority of God. But My power is so great that My creatures cannot come close to Me and behold the beauties of My character.

God, the Son, took the role of coming to the creatures in the form of a creature, having put aside His unapproachable glory. Then the creatures could behold the beauties of His character as He lived among them, as one of them. And it's on the Cross that My character, the character of Jesus, and the character of the Holy Spirit was so clearly portrayed, because Our love is truly unselfish, completely and thoroughly unselfish...and that was demonstrated in that Jesus was willing to give up *Himself* completely. He was willing to sacrifice *everything* for the good of His creatures. And so, that's why He said, if you've seen Me, you've seen the Father, because I have that same unselfish love as Jesus and the Holy Spirit does as well.

Now, the Holy Spirit, He chose the role of the One who would put aside glory and majesty and power, but He also put aside a visible presence and be the invisible presence of divinity that can work with *every single person at the same time.* He's not just on the throne of heaven, and He's not just in Jerusalem the way Jesus was. Instead, He's able to be with everybody and work with every human being at the same time—loving everyone, working with them, and drawing them with love and truth and trying to help them to understand that We divine beings can be trusted and that if you will trust Us, We will do wonderful things for you.

I hope this isn't too complicated, but it's not an easy thing to portray because there's really nothing like Us exactly on Earth.

Now, one of the things that We planned for when We created this world was to help the universe understand a little bit more how the Three can be One.

When We created humanity as male and female, this was planned so that the onlooking universe could see that here are two creatures who are very much alike, yet have some differences, but coming together they can become one...and their oneness can lead to creation. And that's what We want the universe to see—that We are One and yet separate...or distinct individuals, but it's Our Oneness in our character, Our principles of unselfish love that lead to the creation of truly free, intelligent beings who can love and who can interrelate with Us almost as equals. That's what We want the universe to understand.

Two human beings, a man and woman who do become one, *glow* in their oneness and can understand each other just by a look. They don't even have to talk. And their sharing of values, affection, the meaning of life, and their goals and so on, can become so unified that they can even start to look like each other over the years. So this hopefully helps human beings, as well as the onlooking universe, to understand some parts of this concept of three distinct persons and yet all One.

The main thing is We want you to know that We love you. Each of you are a distinct creation. We made you so there's no one else *anywhere* exactly like you. And because you are Our work of art, so to speak, Our own precious creation, you are indeed precious to Us, and We love you, and We will never do anything to hurt you. We will only work for your good, to build you up, to help you, to make you be all that you can be, really. And that's what We want.

You asked who will come when Jesus is comes again. Truly, *Jesus* is coming again.

If you read there in John, chapter 14, Jesus promised, "I'm going to prepare a place for you, and *I will come again* to receive you to Myself."

In Acts, chapter 1, the angel said to the disciples who watched Jesus ascend up into heaven, "*This same Jesus will come again.*" Of course, Jesus, in Matthew 24, describes a lot about His personal coming to the Earth. And then in First Thessalonians, chapter 5, Jesus is described as coming again, and the saved people of Earth are caught up into the air to meet the Lord and to go to the homes that He has prepared.

Then in Revelation, chapters 20, 21 and 22, it talks about how the saved will be in that heavenly home, the new Jerusalem, and they will see Jesus and they will see God, they will see Me…that's a time when I will be able to unveil My glory and the saved people will not be hurt by that glory, they will instead be invigorated by it and be able to enjoy My presence, because they will understand that I have that same character as Jesus does. And that's something I'm looking forward to…in fact, in the scriptures I've said that *that's a day that I am going to sing.* I am going to sing at the joy of having My whole family together. And I am looking forward to that day.

Male, 22, Madison, Wisconsin:
Dear God, what are the winning lottery numbers?

Ha, ha, ha. Oh, you remind Me of a man who came running up to Jesus and interrupted what Jesus was teaching that day, and he said, "Lord, Lord, tell my brother that he has to share his inheritance with me! He's not being fair!" And Jesus said, "Who made Me a judge over you concerning this?"

Jesus went on to talk about how the love of money is a real problem. Jesus hadn't come to settle issues about money. Money is a temporary thing. And, you want the winning lottery numbers—the winning lottery numbers are not going to solve your problems. In fact, they'll probably increase your problems. If this is your one question that you want to ask Me, you have some real problems…problems of not having the best priorities in your life…not having the greatest set of values. So I would encourage you to put aside the lottery and other things that would promise a quick dollar, and instead take some time to consider the important issues of life. What are the things that are going to last, not only for this life but for eternity? Pursue those things. And *those are* the real winning lottery numbers.

Female, 17, Beijing, China:
Dear God, will the world end in a nuclear war?

There's a place in the Bible, in Revelation, that says when Jesus returns He will destroy *those who would* destroy the Earth.

So the Bible does allow for the thought that man has the capacity to destroy the Earth. I am not surprised by that. I knew this ahead of time...like everything else. So I have anticipated this *challenge*, this situation, and have given evidence in *My Word* that people do not need to be afraid that this will take place.

When Jesus was there, He said, "Blessed are the meek, for they shall inherit the Earth." That's in Matthew 5.

So, the Earth will be inhabited, in eternity.

Isaiah talks about how people, and the Earth made new, will be able to build new homes and have vineyards and *enjoy* real life on Earth.

Heaven, or eternal life, is not floating on a cloud strumming a harp and singing with the angels. Heaven is a real existence, a real life on an Earth made new.

Now, Jeremiah, chapter 4, does describe an Earth that is empty of living people, an Earth that has its cities in destruction. Desolation everywhere...over the whole face of the Earth. Which would look like a scene from a movie that describes a nuclear holocaust that engulfs the world. However, what will produce that scene, that condition of the world, is not a nuclear holocaust, but instead, will be the actual coming of Christ. His return. And that's described in a few different places in the New Testament. One place speaks of how the "*brightness of His coming*" will destroy the unbelieving people. And in Revelation, chapter 6, it talks about the coming of Jesus and describes those who are not in tuned with Him—they're crying for the mountains and the rocks to fall on them, and hide them from the face of Jesus. And then, in Revelation 19, it describes Jesus coming on a white horse with all the army in heaven…and He comes forth to conquer the wicked. I don't like to use that term because *all* humans are sinners. *Unbelievers* is a better term, because they are only lost because they refused to believe in My goodness, and that I was really offering them eternal life as a free gift. They wouldn't accept it. So unbelievers is a better term. And they're all destroyed, there in Revelation 19.

And then, Jesus said in Matthew 24 that His coming would be like the days of Noah, where some were taken and some were left. And of course, in the days of Noah, the *flood* took away all of the unbelievers. And the ones who were left were the few people who believed in Me and who were safe in the Ark. They were preserved, alive.

And so, at the coming of Jesus, the believers will be preserved, *alive*. They will be, as Paul said, in 1 Thessalonians, chapter 4, caught up in the clouds to be with Jesus, and they will go with Him to what was prepared for them.

And the lost, the unbelievers, will be destroyed by the brightness of His coming and by the mountains falling, and all of the turmoil that will take place in the world. They will be destroyed and left dead. And they will be left dead for a thousand years, as Revelation 20, describes it. Satan will be bound here on this desolate Earth to be bored...just to *think* about all of the terrible things that he has done for over six-thousand years. And no human beings will be alive on Earth. Saved ones will be in heaven with Jesus, doing some important things there. On Earth, there will be nothing but Satan and his evil angels to think about all of the havoc they've caused...and for what? I told them ahead of time, it's going to be useless; to hold onto sin and selfishness will only lead to agony, to frustration, to pain, to suffering, and death. And they will see that it's true. But, unfortunately, it won't change them.

And so, don't be afraid of nuclear holocaust, I'm not going to *allow* that to take place. I have something *much different*, *much better* in mind. And you don't have to be among those who will be left in this desolate world, left dead here. You can be among those who will enjoy eternity.

<u>Female, 19, College Student, Portland, Oregon:</u>
Dear God, was Darwin's Theory correct?

Well...you're asking *Me* if Darwin's theory was correct, but maybe it would be better to start by asking Darwin. You see, before he died, he made some statements to the effect that he saw the *error* of his theory.

Darwin was trying to observe My creation and be open minded about the facts and information he was observing. And, there were some aspects of his theory that fit with what he observed. For instance, he saw that there were changes in species in the animal kingdom, and he provided a reasoning and a theory of how those changes took place...and that's true, there are changes that take place, and some of it does have to do with random differences in the genes and chromosomes...but it also has to do with natural selection that results because in this world where sin has entered, and as a result death has entered, selfishness predominates. Then the larger, stronger of the species will often outlast the smaller, weaker ones and can be involved in procreating with their genes, and the strengths in their genes will go on...and so the process of natural selection *is* taking place in the world on a regular basis. I designed the genetics of the things of this world in such a way that this could happen...and it helps so that a species has more adaptability and can deal with the difficulties of life on planet Earth as a result of sin and death. And so I built that in. I designed it so that life can stay as good and as strong as possible, even with this mess that we have to deal with.

However, the problem is that Darwin did what so many human beings are prone to do—he looked no farther than he could see. In other words, he was looking at it from his own perspective, and this was the information he had, and so his *theory* only dealt with the information that he had readily at hand that he could observe, and felt that he had to provide an answer that would suffice with that information alone. And that's a problem, because I have given to mankind, through revelations that have been recorded in the scriptures, that there's more to life, and there's more to planet Earth, there's more to the universe than what human beings can observe. And, you have to take that into account. Now I know it's hard to do that, because how can you know what you haven't observed? And I've only given you partial additional information. So you *can't* answer all the questions that there are. It's frustrating, I know. But, I don't want you to get side-tracked with lots of issues that are not important. Because if you get side-tracked into all those things, then you won't get to deal with the issues *that are* important—issues that deal with the eternal results of choices that people are making here on Earth now—issues about helping people who are in need, and making a difference in their lives, and lifting up the burdened and giving hope to the hopeless, and encouragement to the discouraged...and just making a positive difference in people's lives that affect them, not only now but for eternity. That's what I really want you to get involved in.

So...I hope you won't make that mistake Darwin made in having too limited of a vision. *Expand* your view, your mind...let it be *really* opened. I've got a lot to share with you if you'll do that.

Female, 10, Kuwait City, Kuwait:
Dear God. Where are You?

Where are You? Hmmm, such a simple question. Where are You?

Well, you are so precious to Me that wherever you are is where I want to be. At home, at school, at your grandparents' house, when you're away on vacation, wherever you go, I'm watching over you—and not only that, I'm right there with you, ready to enjoy you...and I *hear* your prayers and I really enjoy that. I want to protect you and help you in any way that you need. Of course, I do have all of the universe to care for...but I have some special abilities to care for all of that; at the same time, I'm right there with you. It's hard to explain, but that's not important. Just like how a TV works is hard to explain. But you don't have to understand all of the details to enjoy it. And so I hope that you can enjoy Me and My love and My care for you even though I can't explain it all to you. But do know that it's as if you're the only one in all the world and I hear your every prayer, and every time you wake up, I'm watching over you, and every time you go to bed and all through the day, I've got My eye on you...and I'm smiling from above...and I'm very close to you, too. You can depend on Me.

Male, 34, U.S. Senator, Washington D.C.:
Dear God, is Satan a Republican or a Democrat? And Your leaning???

You mean you want Me to mix politics and religion? You want Me to get into trouble again, huh?

When Jesus was crucified He was brought before religious leaders, and then, the government leaders. And there's always been trouble when you mix politics and religion, in the whole history of the world. Well, Satan doesn't mind doing that—he is *both* a Republican and a Democrat. Because he will use whomever he can to accomplish what he desires. In fact, he is both a Protestant and a Catholic. He is both a Jew and a Gentile. He is both black and white. He is both rich and poor. He is both educated and ignorant. He will go into any philosophy, any institution, any social group, any race, and he will cause as much trouble as he can from that vantage point.

And as for My leaning...the question implies that I would be involved in the human forms of government, and settling of issues, and so on. If you read My Word, in the writings of the profit Isaiah, chapter 48, you will find that he wrote for Me that My ways are not your ways. My ways are above your ways. In fact, as high as the heavens are above the Earth, so are My ways higher than your ways.

So, neither Democrat nor Republican comes anywhere near what I would like to do with humanity and with human governments. Now, the book of Daniel, chapter 7, talks about how the governments of this world will be completely destroyed and blown away, and I will set up My kingdom, a kingdom that will *never* be destroyed and will never perish. It will last forever.

So…don't feel like either the Democrats or the Republicans have all the answers. *I* have the answers…and I'm glad you're asking Me the questions.

Female, 28, Actress, New York:
God, there was a steel Cross that formed in the rubble of the World Trade Center. Did You put that there?

Did I put that there? This is a difficult one.

I'm not going to answer that right now.

Does it make a difference whether I put that there or not? The important thing is, that you saw it, that others saw it, and it made them think.

You thought of a Cross from two thousand years before, and you thought of one person who died. Here in the midst of a tragedy where thousands died, you thought of One who had died. At a time when people died with no accusation against them, you thought of One who died and was accused. In the midst of a time when thousands died who were considered innocent, you thought of One who died because He was condemned. You thought of One who considered Himself divine. And you thought of One who rose from death...One who said that He had the power of life to share with others, and had demonstrated it. That's the important thing. That many here in this time, two thousand years after Christ, are still thinking of Him and considering His claims and finding hope when all seems hopeless, and meaning when things seemed meaningless. And *that's* the important thing.

Now, someday I want to tell you about a lot of the *details* of this world and this life, of what I did and what I didn't do, and when I acted and why I acted, and why I waited sometimes. There a lot of things I want to share with you, and it's going to take a long time, but I promise you it's going to be interesting. And, I think that's the best time for Me to tell you about whether it was Me or not that put that Cross there.

In the meantime, keep looking to the Cross. There's more there than meets the eye. I think I'll leave it at that.

Female, 13, Bangkok, Thailand:
If You are God, what do You look like?

What's this *if*? I *am* God. And, I can't say that I look like anything because you can't see Me right now. I can't *let* you see Me right now. If I were to allow you to see Me you would die. You would perish. I explained this to Moses, —No man can see Me and live.

What I meant was that the glory and power that emanates from My being is just *so* tremendous and awesome that it destroys anything that is out of harmony. And right now you're not in harmony with Me. You still have a sinful human nature. You still have ideas and motives that are not pure. Sin is very much a part of you—as it is of every human being. And that's been My great challenge—how to save human beings, be close to them, and allow them close to Me, to behold Me and to come into My presence, the presence of My glory and power, and yet not be destroyed. I don't want you to be destroyed, so that's why you can't see Me now, because we're in this whole process whereby you can be changed, you can be transformed, you can be cleansed, and you can be purified. It takes several steps—one of the things you need to understand is My love…and that's why Jesus came and died and He paid the whole price of your sins so that the record of your sins against you can be wiped out and you can look and see the great love that I have, that I would even go to the Cross for you…and you can respond to that love with appreciation. As you appreciate and admire Me, you become changed and come into My likeness, and in My likeness, in Me, there is no sin. So, as you become changed more into My likeness, you're purified of sin; even your sinful motives are transformed. You become a new creature. Another step is when Jesus returns and completely changes your nature so that you no longer have a sinful nature. And then you have an opportunity to understand the whole process of how I've dealt with sin. Through all of this you come into more and more and more harmony with Me. The sin and the doubts and the questions are all cared for. Then there will come a time when, as Revelation 22 says, "And you *will* see Me."

When you see Me, *then* you'll see what I look like. And I'm not going to say more, except that I described in Genesis 1, right at the beginning of the Bible, when man and woman were created they were made in My likeness according to My image.

So, though sin has come in, you still bear some likeness to Me. How much? Well, you'll find that out one day. Just let Me take you through all of those steps. Trust Me. I can do it. And, one day you will see for yourself.

Male, 29, Copenhagen, Denmark:
Dear God…Why are the Jews always being persecuted?

To understand why they're being persecuted, you need to first understand who the Jews are. They come from Abraham, the descendents of Abraham. I told Abraham—no, I didn't just tell him, I promised him—it's found in Genesis, chapters 12 and onward—I promised him that I would make of him a great nation, which is where the Jews come from. So that's who the Jews are—that great people. But more significantly, not just that I would make them a lot of people—an influential people, powerful people—but I said to Abraham that I, through him and his descendents, would bless *all the families* of the Earth. Now, this is such an important thing for you to be aware of...that My intention was not to just bless Abraham, but *through him* I could bless *all* the families of the Earth. So, I really wanted to bless *everyone*, and that's why in the Gospel of John, chapter 3:16, it says, "For God so loved *the world* that He gave His only begotten Son..."

My intention has always been to save *as many people of the world*, from *all different backgrounds*, *all races* as possible. Now, the way that I chose, for various reasons, was that I wanted to work through a nation—a large group of people. People who could, first of all, know Me well, and then they could share the truth about Me with *the world*. So first of all, I needed to have a leader of that people who, himself, would know Me well. And this is where Abraham comes into the picture, because of all the people in the world at that time, *he* was the one who wanted to know Me well. So, I was ready to work with him, and build him and his experience and his faith in Me so that he could share it with his family and servants and descendants. Then I could have a whole nation who could know Me well and understand My ways, who could apply My principles to their lives and then reveal Me to the world. And people of the world could come to this nation, this body of people, and they could not only *hear* about Me, My ways, My truths, My government and My character, but they could *see* My character manifest in their lives and in the way they did government, the way they did social interactions, and religious observances, and in every aspect of life, really. So that's why when I took the Jewish people out of Egypt, through the leadership of Moses, and brought them toward the Promised Land, why I gave to Moses, to share with the people, a large variety of commandments and statutes that they could live by—things that dealt with the economy, social interaction, family, health, cleanliness, religious worship...and every aspect of life. And if they had followed... Well, My plan was for them to follow those things, and then the nations of the world could come and find a very good representation of Myself...and it would be one that would win the trust and love and worship of many people of the world. This plan of Mine began to be fulfilled in the time of Solomon. People were coming from all over the world and were learning from Solomon, his wisdom and his insight; they were learning from the government and the social interaction as the people were applying a good portion of the counsel that I had given them. So it came very, very close to a fulfillment at that time. However, then Solomon got involved with so many wives, and then their religions, and the whole thing fell apart. And, really, Israel never recovered from that.

Then, when Jesus came to give a personal manifestation of God—now God in the flesh—unfortunately the nation of Israel, the Jewish people, were not in harmony with Me, not even enough to recognize who Jesus was and to accept Him. Instead, they rejected Him and His ways and His teachings. Although there were many *who did* accept...but it wasn't the largest portion and it wasn't the leaders...so I had to take the portion who did believe, that is, the twelve disciples and their followers, and begin a *new* movement in the world—now a church, instead of a nation, Christianity. All that background—that's important for you to understand.

If you go back to Deuteronomy, chapters 28–30, you'll find that when I took the Jewish people at their very beginning as a nation to the Promised Land, I gave to Moses what is often called *the blessings and the cursings.* I explained to the people that if they truly followed Me there would be all of these wonderful things that would happen, as I had just described. But then I also warned them that if they did not follow Me, and if they turned away and became rebellious, and if they refused to follow and to believe the possibilities of that which I had placed before them, then they would lose all of those blessings, and more than that there would be *curses* upon them, which is basically the natural result of not having the blessings. Just as if a person doesn't have any *good* food, then they have only poor food, or, starvation. So, since the Jewish people rejected the truth and all the good things that go along with following Me, then, all there was left was the bad stuff.

This hurt Me very much, as was expressed by Jesus when He wept over Jerusalem. It hurt very much to have to honor the free choice of the Jewish people and their leaders as they turned away from Me, knowing that all this trouble was going to come upon them. But, just as any parent has to be consistent, so I had to be consistent with My *Word* and My principles. I had to honor that choice and let them go into lots of trouble. Part of the warning was that they would be persecuted wherever they went, and it would be very, very awful. And it's not that I turned from loving them to hating them. That's not it at all. Indeed, in a way I loved them *all the more* because I hurt so much for them. But they put themselves outside My protection...and so, Satan, who loves to try to ruin all My plans and loves to deface any of My creation, set upon this created nation of Mine, this specially beloved people of Mine. He set upon them to deface them, to ruin them, to cause as much pain and anguish to them as possible, knowing that through that he would hurt Me. And it's been awful. I will be glad when that comes to a complete end. I still look forward to winning many of the Jewish people to believe in the truth about Me...and be a part of My eternal kingdom, based on truth and freedom and love. There will yet be many. I'm sure of it. I know it. And I'm glad of it.

Female, 22, Waitress, Nashua New Hampshire:
What do You call Yourself in Your inner thoughts?

Through the prophet Isaiah, I expressed that My thoughts are above your thoughts and My ways are above your ways. And so, it's a very great challenge to try to help you to understand My thoughts. When you deal with certain situations in your family, for instance, you try to consider everyone in the family. You don't want to do something for one person that would *hurt* somebody else. And so you try to think above the parents and the children and so on...and try to take in as many of the people and protect everyone's feelings and work for the good of all. My family is not only *all* of humanity, the more than six billion people, but there's also the family in heaven, the unfallen angels, and then, inhabited worlds around the universe who are all part of the picture that I have to consider. So, I'm able to take in all of that and deal with all of it. That may help you to get a picture that My thoughts and ways have to be much bigger and broader and all-encompassing. And so, at this point I really can't share with you more than what I have said in the scriptures in the Bible, when I said to Moses —*I am* the I am.

That is an open-ended statement. When Jesus was here He helped to give some elements of the completion of that thought. He said, I am the truth, I am the way, I am the life, and the resurrection, and many other things. So just take those elements that you find in the Bible and be open to more and more and more of them. I think *that* perhaps is the best that I can do to help you start to get an idea of how I see Myself. And I'm really sure that as you learn more and more about Me to complete that thought of *I am*, I'm really sure that you'll be able to love Me and trust Me more and more. And we can have a really neat friendship together. Because *I am* the one who loves you.

Male, 35, La Paz, Bolivia:
Why are there only 24 hours in a day?

You *couldn't handle* any more than that.

Female, 36, Moscow, Russia:
Dear God — Why does life seem so hard at times?

I know it does seem hard at times. And it not only seems hard at times, it *is* hard at times—I know that. And it's hard for Me, too.

If you look at the experience of Jesus in Gethsemane and His experience on the Cross, you get a taste of how hard it has been for Me since the very beginning of this whole problem of sin and selfishness, from the very moment that Lucifer began his rebellion.

Remember Lucifer was My beloved angel, the highest one, the one closest to the throne, the one trusted with the most, the most talent, the most knowledge, the most understanding, the most responsibilities…and, I loved him. It has hurt to see him latch onto something that would bring about his ruin, and that would spread for so many. Even though the Three of us, Father, Son, and Holy Spirit, had already anticipated this problem and had the plan to enact and to bring about a solution, eventually. But, those struggles in Gethsemane and on the Cross show that it's been a struggle for Me from the beginning. And it's hard. It's hard to watch My children hurt. It's hard to not be able to intervene when I want to and when I'd love to. It's been hard not to stop all this mess and this hurt and this pain, and all the struggle that all My children have to go through. But if I were to stop it, it wouldn't really stop. It wouldn't really *solve* the problem—if I were to cut it short. I've got to allow the whole thing to take place. It's absolutely necessary for the problem of sin to be worked out completely, so that the *destruction* of sin—and all who are determined to be connected with it—can be complete and final…and that is going to be a massive step for the universe, and it has got to be done right, and it's got to be done *completely*…so that sin will *never rise up again*. This is the only way. So life is tough—for now. One day it won't be. One day when sin is done with completely and obliterated from the universe, then life will not be tough one moment, one second. There will be joy, there will be peace, there will be fulfillment, there will be freedom, there will be *love*—like never before. And *it will not be marred* one bit. I am intent, I am fully committed, and I have put *everything on the line* so that can happen. And it's going to happen. I want to share that with you and as many others as possible. I want you to be there that day. Together we can say, "It was worth it. All the struggle, all the pain, all the heartache...it was worth it. Because now we have each other, in eternity."

Let's be there together.

Male, 7, Dayton, Ohio:
Hello God. Why does gum lose its flavor?

Well, you haven't tasted the gum in heaven!

Lots of things in this world lose their flavor—you'll find that out all too soon. But I have things planned that will never lose their flavor. I have flowers planned that will never die. I have animals that won't be afraid. I have all kinds of foods planned that are *so* delicious, and pets that will be so much fun to play with, they will never get tired. I've got lots of good stuff, stuff that will never go bad, stuff that will *always* delight you. So, plan on coming to *My* house someday! I've got a plan for you to come. I want you to plan to be there. And we're going to have the best of times together, you and Me. I'm looking forward to it.

Female, 31, Wilmington, Delaware:
God... Why can't I control myself when it comes to eating?

What you're facing is something that is not unusual at all. And, indeed, it goes way back to the very first temptation of mankind. The very first *act of rebellion* on the part of mankind was to eat when he didn't need to eat. Adam and Eve were told to stay away from the tree and not to eat from the fruit of it, and if they did, that's when the problems would begin. Of course, the serpent beguiled Eve and deceived her into thinking it was something good, and she went ahead and ate it in spite of what I told her. She really lost *trust* in Me and My Word when she chose to take that action. Then she brought it to Adam, and Adam didn't trust Me enough to come to Me with the problem when he recognized what Eve had done. He just went ahead and joined her in eating from the fruit. And *eating* has been a problem ever since.

People have gotten themselves into all kinds of trouble with wrong eating. Eating too much, drinking too much, eating the *wrong* things, drinking the wrong things... Even Noah, after the flood, got involved with drinking the wrong things. Lott had a similar problem. And all down through the ages we can see that this was a problem...and continues to be, of course.

Now, when Jesus came—God the Son, He had to face the same temptations that you do. In fact, He faced *every* temptation. He was tempted in every point as you are. And, the very first temptation He faced in the wilderness right after His baptism concerned eating. In the wilderness He had been fasting for forty days, so He was very hungry, very weak, and when Satan appeared to Him, (*not* as a devil, but as an angel from heaven) and said, "Now, if you are the Son of God, go ahead and change the stones into bread and eat, because heaven wants You to survive here." Jesus recognized when this being said "*if* You are the Son of God" that it was an expression not of confidence that would come from heaven, but an expression of doubt that comes from the other place, from the other side. And so He recognized this and He said, "Man shall not live by bread alone, but by every word that proceeds out of the mouth of God." In other words, "I'm going to trust God *more* than I'm going to try to fulfill My need for food, even when My life seems to be on the line here because I'm starving." And so, He won where Adam failed, because Adam trusted himself and the food more than he trusted Me and My Word. So, Jesus expressed that trust and the obedience as a result. And it was on food. It was on temptation. And so, because Jesus was *victorious* on the issue of food, *you* have that victory. Jesus obtained the victory, not for Himself, but He obtained that victory *for you*, for every son and daughter of Adam and Eve. He did it for you. Just as your sins were placed upon Jesus when He went to the Cross, so His righteousness is available for you.

In Second Corinthians 5, verse 21, it says that that's the exchange I want to make for you. I want you to let go of your sin because Jesus already bore them, He took the penalty, and I want you to accept His righteousness because He was earning it all during His whole lifetime of perfect righteousness on every point, including control regarding food—that is yours—it's on your account.

If you could look in heaven and see the record book—so to speak—you would see under *your name* is already registered a life of *perfect control regarding food.* So you already have that if you'll accept that by faith...believing that I love you that much, that Jesus loves you that much, that perfect righteousness of Jesus, His victory over eating problems, that is all recorded for you. You don't have to earn it. You don't have to try to impress Me with your carefulness regarding food. But, now, if you'll let Me, I will come along and lift you up to obedience. I will lift you into an experience where you will no longer have a necessity for over-indulgence in food. You will have new motivations of wanting to use your time, money, strength and abilities—not to satisfy your own selfish desires—instead, you'll want to do that which would be an honor to Me, because you appreciate My love and My goodness. But also, you'll want to use all that you have to preserve your health for the good of helping other people. Because, the less strength you have and the less health you have, the less you can be a blessing to others. And I want to put such an attitude of unselfishness in you that you will just naturally turn away from that kind of eating that is unhealthy or self-centered, and you can eat for the good things that you are, and preserve a health that can bless others and bring honor to Me.

I really want you to be healthy. Without health there's so little in life that you can enjoy. I want you to be healthy and strong, and to enjoy life as much as you can. So, stay close to Me and trust Me, and I will lead you into abundant life, just as Jesus said. That's what I want—for you.

Male, Caracas, Venezuela:
Dear God – How do You feel about being asked so many questions?

Oh, I love it. I enjoy it. It's a delight. And you can tell when you look at the life of Jesus. Many people came and asked Him questions, and often He would answer with another question. He enjoyed interacting with people. He especially liked it when people asked questions that showed a sincere desire to learn. He was just so thankful that people wanted to learn, that they had open minds, and they were searching, looking for answers…especially answers to the really big questions in life. And certainly, that's how I feel…just as Jesus said, "If you've seen Me, you've seen the Father." So, I feel exactly the same way. Notice also when you look at Jesus, when people asked Him smart-alecky questions, He would turned things around either with another question or just a different approach. He would turn it around so that

He would almost make them *think* some serious thoughts and ponder important issues, even if they were just trying to mess with Him, so to speak. So, I'm glad for each question, and I think it's great for the opportunity to interact with *you*...and with each person.

Male, 22, Boston, Massachusetts:
Dear God,
Everyone always asks where were You when such and such happened...like where were You when Kennedy got shot? Because this is my generation, my question is: God, where were You on 9/11?

Well...this is a question that *others* have been asked. And some have attempted answers. And some of those answers have been pretty good. The daughter of Billy Graham responded, "You've taken God out of our schools and universities and courts and businesses and many of our homes, and now you have the nerve to ask where He was?" Someone else gave an answer along the line that I was there with the people who were rescuing, with the heroes in the airplane who prevented a fourth crash that would have caused more casualties; I was in the homes and in the subways causing delays to make people late for work so that there would be fewer people in the Trade Center that day, with the people who were there but stayed calm and helped direct things so that a vast number of people were able to get out of the buildings before they collapsed, with the people who should've been on those planes but weren't, (usually the planes that flew out at that time on those flights on those mornings are rather full and on this day they were considerably empty).

But, you mentioned that it's not just that one occasion, there are *many* occasions when humans ask where *I* was when the tragedy was taking place? And, I really wish that I could stop *all* hurt and pain and tragedy and all death and all evil of this world. I wish I could. I wish I could've, right at the beginning just stopped it and not let it even happen. But, *that* would be an even greater tragedy, because then there would be no real freedom.

The license plate of the State of New Hampshire says, *Live free or die*. And that shows that there have been people, in various times, certainly the ones who were in New Hampshire, but there have been people in different places in different times who have recognized and even put into words that, *if there is no freedom—then there is no sense in living*. And as the creator, I would say it this way...*if there is no real freedom for My creatures, there would be no sense in creating them.*

When I decided to create intelligent, free creatures, I made a commitment to do whatever it took to cherish and to protect that freedom. And I am not going back on that commitment, not one bit. To Me it will be worth it. All that I've done, all that I've suffered, all that I've hurt...because I hurt when every one of My creatures hurts, when every human child or person hurts. But it's been worth it all, even if *you* were the only one in all the world who responded...I would go through it all for you. Your freedom is that valuable to Me, and I will *enjoy* you for eternity. We'll have a special time together for eternity because you're *really* free. That's what I want.

Male, 44, Postal Worker, Miami-Dade, Florida:
God, it might sound petty, but my vote back in the 2000 election was not counted...and every time I see the President I relive my anger. I'm mad as hell, I feel ripped off, and I feel Bush stole the election. Was that whole election "just politics"? Did I, and the American public, get screwed? And why can't I seem to let it go?

You're asking for Me to unveil what I am doing and not doing behind the scenes of life, and in this case, political life specifically, and of the leadership of the United States. I think that that's not the best for Me to do.

I *have* revealed in the Bible that I set up kings and that I take down kings...and that the nations of the Earth are in My hands. You can know that I am involved in the direction of the nations and who comes into leadership. Of course the United States is a very important part of leadership in this world at the present time. So, you can be assured that I am involved *when* and *where* I feel I need to be. Therefore, perhaps I *was* overruling events in that election. But, I may not have been. I may have *allowed* the political process to run its course because it was not needful for Me to intervene. And whether I did intervene, whether I did not, you'll have to leave that up to Me. And that's really what I'm asking of you and other Americans and other human beings is that you come to know My ways and purposes and goals and procedures...to the extent that you trust Me and that you trust what I do and what I don't do, to trust My wisdom to know when to act and when not to, to trust that I always have your good in mind, and the good of everyone, the best that can be done in the circumstances, without destroying anyone's ultimate freedom.

Now, you *feel* shortchanged, robbed of your vote. You must look at it this way—you did everything that you could do. You went to the polls. You thought about it ahead of time and with that planned decision you acted and voted. You did your part. The fact that those in charge of the voting did not proceed with the best preparations and the best way of carrying out the counting, and therefore your vote was not counted correctly or at all—you have to let go of that. Leave it with *them*, just as you have to leave many other things with other agencies, and bureaucrats, and leaders...and ultimately, you have to leave it with Me. So, put your trust in Me and in My power to control things where it's needed. Remember that the things of this world are passing away quickly. Really, this is a small thing in the big picture. Take My Word again, and as you read the Bible, look for the bigger view, the view that takes in not only current events, but the whole world history. The view that takes in not only this world, but the whole universe. Not only the issues of *your* life, but the issues of the great controversy between good and evil that pervades *all* that's been happening in this world since its beginning, and how *that* needs to be resolved, and not only in the universe and in this world but in *your heart.* And consider those big issues and where you stand with those things. When you resolve that, and when you resolve what place I have in your life and in your heart, that will care for the disturbance that you feel over this voting issue. I'm sure it will help.

Now, when it comes to you being angry, continually, at Mr. Bush...you need to let go of that, and instead, I really would like you to pray *for* him. Mr. Bush is a man...he's not perfect. He's not perfectly good nor perfectly evil. And no leader, no potential President would be perfect. But he is a man, and he has some good points and some weaknesses, but now that he is in office, and while he is in office, there are things that I would like to do *through* him. When you pray, and when others pray for him, it gives Me the invitation to get more involved in what I can do for him, and through him, for the benefit of many others. So, when you're tempted to be angry, instead, turn to Me about that and express your anger to Me, let *Me* take it...and then pray for him that he would have an attitude to let Me use him and that I would be able to do greater things through him. And then let's see how *we* can work together to make things better.

Male, 74, Retired Doctor, Phoenix, Arizona:
I got to tell you, God, I don't know where I stand with You. When my father was 62…he was a lousy driver, he went one day with my mother to get his license renewed, and he took the test, they gave him a hard time, but anyway, he got it. He was going to drive away…and all of a sudden, boom, he died of a heart attack. Now, what's the purpose of that? The guy never hurt anybody. A great guy. You got all these CEO's and all these bastards raising hell, and the CEO's ripping off everybody…I mean, what are You there for? WHO are You there for? Are you there just for the good things? I just don't understand that.

I understand your confusion and your pain. The tragedy, the unfairness, especially the inhumanity of man towards man in this sinful world has hurt Me from the beginning. In fact, the anguish that you see Jesus enduring on the Cross gives you just the smallest taste of how hurt I have been for over six thousand years. But, being hurt isn't enough. *Doing something* is crucial, as your question implies. And I perceive that *you* do not see what I am doing. Or, you don't understand that I am doing anything. But don't forget the Cross. The Cross was not suffering, alone. It certainly was suffering, but, there was *vic-*

tory there. *The Cross was the greatest victory there ever has been or ever will be* of good over evil. Now, it doesn't look like it because Jesus died...but when He rose again and ascended into heaven and stood before Me and the onlooking universe and asked if the sacrifice was enough, if He had accomplished everything that the plan of salvation called for... That I Myself, together with all of the intelligent beings of the unfallen universe, could say, "*It was more than enough.*" And so, not only have I done *some*thing, I have done *everything* that's needed to bring about the end of sin. Sin *will* end—that's what the Cross says. Sin, suffering, unfairness, sickness, death *will end.* It's an absolute certainty now. The question is the *timing.*

Now, some think that I'm slack or too slow concerning the fulfillment of My promise. But, I'm not just being slack or too patient...I want as many as possible to be saved. And, that's what I'm doing. I'm setting things up. I'm allowing the continuation of this world to the point where the final actions that are needed can be taken at such a time and in such a way that *as many as possible* will be able to respond to the truth about Me and the truth about salvation so that as many as possible will *allow Me* to save them. That's what My love demands. That's the love that has secured the end of sin and death...and the security and the ultimate happiness and the eternal freedom and safety of the universe, forever.

So...you need to look further than events in your

family. You need to see more in order to understand the 'whys' of what's happened to your dad and all. If you go to My Word, the answers are there. The bigger picture is there. The ultimate victory of good and fairness and love is there. That's why My Word is so important. It has the big answers to the big questions. So, go there. And, as you're reading, I will send the Holy Spirit to you, to help you to understand, to put it together. Not only to find the answers—but to find Me. Because I want you to know Me...and we can enjoy each other for eternity.

Male, 29, Pro Football Player, Manchester, England:
Dear God... What is the purpose of Stonehenge? Who built it? And why?

Stonehenge is just one of many locations around the world where ancient peoples set up large stone structures to enhance their worship of the gods. There were various aspects to those religions and reasons why structures were made the way they were.

If you go back to the book of Genesis and you read what was happening just before the flood, and just after with the Tower of Babel, you'll get as much information as you really need on this. Because it tells how people used the wonderful mental capacities that I've given them, which, back at that time, had not been degenerated very much by sin. They were more mentally sharp than humans are today, but they took that great ability, as well as their great physical abilities, and instead of using them for good and to enhance their knowledge and love of Me and of one another, and seeking to share their burdens and help one another, they got involved in deceptive and violent and evil things. I am not going to talk about the aspects of their religion and the purposes of those structures, because I practice what I ask of you. And I've asked of you, as expressed by Paul in Philippians 4:8, that you choose to think on those things which are pure and right and good, just and holy. So I don't want to turn your thoughts toward all the evil, the immorality, and the violence of their religion and culture. But, you can see there in Genesis that I had to deal with that then, and, of course, right on through the ages until the present day. You can see *how* I dealt with it, and that just as I gave the people opportunities to turn from their rebellious and wickedness, I gave opportunities to turn towards that which brings *life* and *light* into life. So, today, that's what I am doing I'm giving people opportunities. I'm working with strength and power, although sometimes subtly and quietly, because that's the best way, the most effective way. I'm working to win people's hearts, to change their lives, to give them a new beginning and a new future and a hope like they've never had before. And *that's* what I want to talk about. Let's talk about hope. Let's talk about the future. Let's talk about the *good* that can last for eternity.

You may be wondering, *Is this place of Stonehenge*

therefore an evil place? Certainly many people go there curious and with awe and are just amazed that the structure could even be built, and then also curious as to why it was built. Some even go there to participate in what little modern man knows about the religion of that time.

Well, I wouldn't say that it's an evil place...certainly it's a historical place, just as the pyramids of Egypt and the structures of the Incas and the other ancient peoples are historical places. And, I wouldn't discourage people from visiting there, or asking questions. Remember, one of the prime aspects of My relationship with you is that I am a teacher. Teachers like questions. At least I do. I *really* like questions. I want people to think—and to reason. I've given reason to you for that purpose, so that you can think things through and come to understand that which is true and right and important. So, I'm glad for people to be curious and to ask questions...but I don't want them to get hung up on those things and get sidetracked from the most important by that which is of so little importance.

Again, I'm hoping that the questions people ask when they go to Stonehenge will lead them to question My existence, and then how I've revealed Myself, and hopefully that will give them a desire to study more about Me from My Word, and then they'll see the *richness* of what I really have to offer human beings today.

Female, 15, Student, Tel Aviv, Israel:
Dear God — Why can't humans live in peace?

Well, there are many aspects to the answer to that question. They have found that one reason people don't live in peace is because they don't take good care of themselves physically. There was an experiment that scientists did a couple of decades ago where they took a group of about twenty women. They had them live together and share a home or facility and they decreased their intake of B vitamin. Other things in their lives were left the same as they lived together for a period of time. They found that the women became irritable with each other and uncooperative and then angry, and then they were fighting. In fact, they fought so much that the experiment was stopped early because it was becoming dangerous.

Well, that shows that one element of human strife is nutrition. Proper nutrition. Not everyone gets that proper nutrition, and that can add to strife. Link that with alcohol and nicotine and drugs of all kinds, and that has a big effect on people's abilities to get along.

There are also other factors, such as lack of sleep, stress, and problems in the home. And then there are just the aspects of human nature—sinful human nature with its selfishness and pride...and with that comes the jealousy and envy, then vengeance and so on. It is quite a mess.

You may have concerns on a personal level or it may be on the national level, but really it goes back to the same things—the nature of man. And that's just the way sin is. Sin leads to strife and heartache and tragedy, and death. When sin is in control, there is no way of stopping that. That's why I want to have control. I don't want to have control just to be the boss, to be the dictator, and have everybody bow down to Me as if they're just My pawns, My slaves. I want to be in control because I want to guide things in ways that lead to life—abundant life—with happiness and joy and without the strife that tears down. I want that which builds up, lifts and strengthens, gives hope and life and delight. That's what I want. That's what I'll always work for. And one day everyone will see that very, very clearly, and I will not let the universe down—that's the way I will be forever. Then there won't be strife. And there won't be all the anguish that goes with it. So I look forward to a day that all things will be under My control, completely. I want you to be there, because you'll be able to say, as David did, "We adore You as being in control of everything."

Female, 41, Denver, Colorado:

Dear God,

I was just watching a discovery show the other night and they were trying to explain the scientific reasons for the plagues, giving reasons for the locust and explaining how a volcano made the lights go dark, instead of by God's hand. Is that true? I mean, are they just making excuses, and why do we see that quite often? It seems there's always a scientific reason for Biblical things. Is man doing that on purpose, or are we just trying to seek the answers? For example – the show said that the Red Sea that parted wasn't really the Red Sea, and that it was mistranslated. How do they know that it was mistranslated? And was it mistranslated? Like the show said that a tidal wave just happened to occur the same time when Moses supposedly parted the sea. That it wasn't really him parting the sea; it was just a tidal wave that came at that time and then swallowed up the people on the chariots. The ten plagues and the Ten Commandments were all explainable. They called it "a figment of a scribe's imagination." What do You have to say?

Remember that *I am the Creator of all things*...all things in this natural world, included. And, I am the designer. I am the One who created everything to function according to certain laws, such as the laws of gravity, the laws of inertia, and so on. Therefore, I know how to use those laws *beyond what man can understand.* And I know how to bring to bear on situations laws *outside* of the realm of what generally operates in the natural world.

Remember that I am not limited by that which limits man. I am not limited by what you see in this world, by what you're able to *observe* in this world. I don't have limits with My knowledge, My wisdom, and what I'm able to do and to use.

There certainly are times when I intervene to accomplish My purposes...and I use the laws of the natural world. For instance, at the time of Noah's flood. At the end of that flood, when I made the covenant with Noah and with all living things that I would not send another flood to kill all life on Earth, I set, as a commemoration of that covenant, *the rainbow* in the sky. It seemed like such a miraculous thing to the people at that time, to see a band of color across the sky. Humans know now that the rainbow effect is simply the refraction of sunlight through the water drops in the sky. And so, now it's a natural phenomena. But, that doesn't make the story of Noah and the flood any less real than when Jesus was on Earth and He took the simple food of the Passover supper—that was real food—He took bread and He took juice, and then He gave it to the disciples in a way that would become a way of commemorating His death for their sins. So, that bread and juice, that Lord's supper, continues down to this day, and it commemorates a very real event, and it was a supernatural event in the sense that a divine human person was dying for the sins of the whole world...but the bread and the juice are *real*, they're common things.

There are other times when I use things that are, I would say, beyond the scope of the natural world as you've been able to observe it. So, I use what I desire to use, what I see is best.

The people who say that there was a mistranslation about the sea which Moses and the Israelites crossed to get out of Egypt...they say that it was the Reed Sea, and that it was really only two or three feet deep. But, it would be pretty amazing to, first of all, have a tidal wave at the precise moment that it was needed, without divine intervention. And then it would be amazing that the whole army of Egypt would be drowned in two feet of water. Maybe that's a greater miracle than having the Red Sea part. Either way, don't try to just explain away My existence and My purposes in the world. You make yourselves look so foolish when there's so much evidence that you have to explain away. Be honest. Be honest with yourself. Be honest with all the evidence that I have placed before you. I'm not asking you to believe in Me, and in My ways, and in My accomplishments like a person leaping into the dark without anything to trust in or to see, with no evidence to base that act upon. I've given you lots of evidence. So much is there. But I'm not going to force you. Therefore, I allow the evidence that can be used to argue against My existence, My ways, and My accomplishments. You have the freedom to choose. I certainly hope you'll choose to know Me.

Female, 42, Fashion Designer, Queens, New York:
If You are so smart—why are there so many different religions? There are so many off-shoots and so forth that create wars, and other troubles—why?

I'm not sure I understand your connection between My smartness, My intelligence, and the problem with human beings in keeping things straight.

One thing that most of modern man has forgotten is the importance of knowing and understanding history.

It would be difficult to discuss the history of *all* religions, but let's deal with the history of those which have relationship to My revealed Word, the Bible, and those would be Christianity and Judaism. If you follow that back you find that I started out with one family—Abraham and his family, and then I worked with them, and later with the nation that resulted from that one family. When you look at that history you see the difficulty that the people had with keeping things straight. For hundreds of years they continued to have the problem of listening to the peoples around them who *did not* have My revealed Word, and they got involved in their religious ideas and brought them into their own worship and got things all mixed up. So I had to punish them and try to get them straight again, over and over again, and then, finally, Jesus came and He accomplished a great deal. But still, the people were using their freedom to choose to stubbornly rebel against what I had revealed to them. So, they rejected their true Messiah. Therefore We had to start another group of people with whom We could work. This was the twelve disciples and the other followers who joined them…and thus the beginnings of the Christian church.

Now look at the first part of Revelation. Chapters 2 and 3 talk about seven letters to seven churches, which are symbolic of the seven eras of Christian church history...and in them you can see that again there surfaced this stubbornness and this tendency to listen to other peoples who do not have My revealed Word, taking their false religious ideas and bringing them into the church...with the result that things went downhill into the dark ages. Then, I was able to get the attention of a few who went back to My Word. The Reformers started to revise the importance of looking to what I revealed in the Bible, and basing faith and their experience with Me *on* what's in the Word.

However, then those Protestant groups began to be afflicted with all of that same stubbornness and...well, it was kind of like a *pride*. They had discovered certain things and they were proud of that and held onto *only* those and would not continue their search for truth. When others did continue, those who maintained a stubborn pride refused to take the next step in the rediscovery of truth. They stayed in their limited position. So, the ones who wanted to take the next step in rediscovering truth had to break away...and so you had a new church form...and so it went, one after another, after another, after another. What I am looking for, and have been working on in recent years, is to bring together a group of people who will look at *all of the truth* that's been discovered so far—no matter what church holds onto that truth—and this group will assemble *all* the truth of My Word, and put it together, and then also have the willingness to be teachable, to *admit* that they don't know everything yet...and they're willing to learn more that I can reveal to them. A teacher doesn't dump everything on their students at once. I reveal it step by step, a little at a time...and there's more for Me to reveal.

I'm looking for, and I've been assembling, people with that attitude. And...very soon I'm going to be able to do some pretty amazing things with those people.

Over the last 150 years I have built a new church movement made up of such people from every nation, language, economic level, and religious background. They have learned important truths from every other church and searched the scriptures to sort the teachings of man and the influences of paganism from the truth of God. They see that all the truths of My Word add something to their understanding of who I am. Because they have accumulated such a large amount of accurate Biblical teaching, they now have the most clear, complete, and consistent picture of Me that anyone has ever had.

You have an inquiring mind—you can be one of them. I want you to be. I'd love for you to have that privilege to share with Me in doing some awesome stuff. Look for the people who "keep the commandments of God and have the testimony of Jesus...which is the spirit of prophecy." —Rev. 12:17, 19:10.

Female, 31, Graphic Designer, Amsterdam, Netherlands: In the galaxies there are millions of stars or planets, and there are possibly billions of people living here and maybe there…so how can You take care of who's good and who's bad and things like that? You must be very busy. How can You know what's going on for all of them? This record, how do You manage that?

This is a difficult question to answer because of the limitations of humanity. You are bound by time and space…and I am not.

Part of divinity is that We are beyond you—beyond your limitations. And I can be free from the boundaries of time that you experience. And so, let Me put it to you this way…there have been books and movies that have been made about people who have been able to travel back in time or forward in time, and you may have come across those books and movies. And what's portrayed is a person, say from the year 2000, will travel back in time to the year 1950, and will experience a variety of things for, we'll say, a period of one month, just to make it simple. After that month of activities, the person will travel forward in time to *the very moment* in the year 2000 when they left. So they will not lose any time in the year 2000, and yet they will have spent a month back in 1950. And then they can go forward in time to the year 2020 and spend a month's time there and still come back and be back in the very same moment, once again in the year 2000. Well, that would be a simplistic way of explaining what I have the ability to do.

I can go back in time, say, to the year that Martin Luther was born...just before 1500. And I could take and spend *a whole lifetime* with Martin Luther, and know him personally, spend every minute of his life with him, watching him, observing him, caring about him, interacting with him, guiding him, helping him, through his whole life...*and then* come back to this very moment...and not have lost one moment of time, so to speak.

Then I could go back to the year Abraham Lincoln was born and spend a whole lifetime with him, and come back and not lose any time.

I could go back to the same time as Martin Luther was born, but spend a whole lifetime *with someone else*, say one of his companions Zwingli or Calvin...spend the whole lifetime with *that* person. And I could do that a billion times. Or a hundred billion times. And, spend a whole lifetime concentrating on one person at a time...and yet, not lose any time. So I could do that for this whole world and every other world because I'm not limited by time. So I can know *every person...* just as if that person was the only one in the whole universe. I can know you that intimately. I can be watching over you, protecting you, answering your prayers, drawing you to My love, guiding you.

In the same way, I have been able to go *ahead* in time. That's why I have been able to tell what's going to happen in the future, because I can go ahead in time and tell what the future holds and I have portrayed that in the scriptures. That's what makes the Bible so unique. But *I don't force* the future. Remember, I'm not into force. I don't *make* the future happen. But I can go into the future, *see* what will happen, and know it. That's why, even before Adam and Eve sinned in the garden, I already had a plan to deal with sin because I knew it was going to happen. Thus, Jesus was described as the lamb slain from the foundation of the world. I looked ahead, in fact, back before the creation of the world, I went ahead in time and I saw what would happen in this world and all of the people who would need to be saved—in fact, *I saw you*. Even before Adam and Eve fell in the Garden, I looked ahead and I saw you. When I determined that the only way that the problem of sin could be resolved was that I would have to die, I saw you and I determined that I would die for you. So when I made that commitment way back in the beginning, that Jesus would die, and together We would suffer for this world, because it was hard for Me to *allow* Jesus to go through with what He did...that was heart-breaking for Me...and the scripture says, "God was in Christ reconciling the world unto Himself." But I saw you—and you were *valuable* to Me. You were worth it. And so, together, We made the determination that we would do it for you...even if you were the only one who would respond, We would go ahead.

You mentioned keeping track of the good people and the bad people. I have to say something about that...because, as I said in the scriptures, *all* have sinned and come short of the glory of God. *All* of humanity has fallen into the grasp of sin. And, really, no one is better than another. That's why Jesus said that I send the sunshine on the just and the unjust...I send the rain on the godly and the ungodly. Really, I don't see your sin. When it comes to accepting and loving you, that's not important to Me because all of you are lost or hurting and affected by this disease of sin. I actually want to help you. I look *past* your guilt and I see your need. And I have the cure for sin; I want to apply that to you in your life and everyone's...if you'll just trust Me, I can do it.

Winning your trust—that's the hard one. I won't force it. But I will do everything I can to win your trust. And I will do as much for one person as if it's for the whole world. And if you were the only one to die for—I would die for you.

<u>Male, 18, Student, South Lancaster, Massachusetts:</u>
Dear God, I am currently in a Christian academy. My question to You is – How can I know if I am going to be saved?

Jesus, speaking to the religious leaders of His day, in Matthew 5, verses 39 and 40, said, "You are searching the scriptures because you think that *in them* you have eternal life. But, *these* are the very things that point to Me, and yet you won't come to Me that *I* could give you life." So, to be in a saved condition, is to be in a saved *relationship*, to be in a close relationship with Me and with Jesus.

In 1 John, it says, "He who has the Son, has life." If you *have* Jesus, if you have accepted Him as the One who loves you more than any other, as the One who paid the ultimate price for your sin and for your redemption from sin and death, if you see that Jesus is really everything to you, because without Him you are nothing, then, if you realize that if you've seen Him, you've seen Me...and so I have that same love for you, that same power; if you have God as your friend and savior and Lord, your teacher, your master...then *you have* eternal life. The gift of life is yours because *you have the One* who *can* and *will*, in fact is *committed* to, giving you life.

So, your question, "How can I know if I will be saved?" is sort of like asking...well, if you have chosen to believe in Our goodness and love and commitment to your salvation, and you have responded by surrendering and inviting Us to accomplish all of that *in* you, if you've done all of that, then, for you to ask, how can you know if you are going to be saved, is sort of like a married man asking, "How can I know that I am married?" Well, if the married person has made his marriage vows and received marriage vows from his wife, we'll say, then, *he is* married. And he's just as married that moment after the vows are complete as he will be fifty years later if they stay married. The key is to stay married. Now, it's not enough to just get married, and the wife goes to Arizona, and the husband goes to Maine, and they live apart for years...that's not real marriage. Real marriage is a relationship of unity.

The Bible says, therefore, the husband shall leave his father and mother and cling to his wife and these two shall become one. And Jesus prayed that his followers would become one with him as he is with Me, the Father.

The *oneness* is so important.

So, the married person, not only has to *get* married, but he has to *stay* married by staying in relationship with his spouse. Similarly, the way you can know that you *will be* saved is to ask: *are you saved now*? Today, have you made that choice? Are you continuing to make it every day? Just continue in relationship, continue responding with faith as you sense Me reaching out to you. I reach out to you first, every day, before you even open your eyes. I'm there watching for you, reaching out to you with love, with caring, with protection, and hoping that you'll notice and that you'll respond with faith and love in return. As you do that every day, you stay in relationship and you have the One who has life—and so *you* have life.

I don't think you yet know how much I love you. But that can be the pursuit of your life—to discover more, and still more, and still more...how much I love you, how much I want you...and *I will not leave anything undone* that needs to be done for you to have eternal life...for you to be saved. You can count on it. You can count on Me.

Male, 33, Bacolod City, Philippines:
How do You choose the people for the TESTS that You give?

There is a place in the scriptures that says, "I will not allow you to be tested with more than you can bear."

I have the ability to know each person inside and out, to know what's in their minds and in their hearts...the deepest recesses of who they are, how they think and feel. I know them better than they know themselves. For instance, I know *you* better than you know yourself.

So, I can see what you can bear better than you can. And there are times when I bring a test upon a person, or I choose a person for a certain test because I recognize that they can bear it. They will succeed through it.

When you think about Abraham...I asked him to offer his only son, Isaac. It was because I knew that Abraham had finally gotten, at that point, to the place where he trusted Me *completely*. I wanted that to be seen, to be demonstrated, not only to mankind, but to the onlooking universe because of the issues of this great controversy between good and evil. And, certainly, Abraham *did* come through that test with flying colors, so to speak.

Then there was Job; he was put on the spot to suffer many and horrible things. But again, it was something that needed to be seen by the onlooking universe because of the accusations that Satan had made against Me and Job—mostly against Me, My government, My ways of doing things. The universe needed to see that Satan was wrong. He had accused Me of gaining the allegiance of Job only by bribery, by sending blessings and providing protection; and should those things be withdrawn then Job's supposed allegiance to Me would evaporate. I knew that was not true. I knew that Job's allegiance to Me was not based upon gifts—but because he knew Me. He understood My ways and appreciated and loved Me and admired Me for them, and that he would trust Me no matter what...and so I allowed Satan to go in and take away everything, and then the onlooking universe could see that the accusations of bribery were totally false. That was *needed* at that time, and it was important that I could count on Job for that.

Of course, you realize that it wasn't Job himself in his own nature that could accomplish that. He was, in his walk with Me, allowing Me to come close to him, indeed inside of him, and I was doing heart surgery on him day by day. I knew that his heart surgery had progressed to the point where it could be demonstrated. So what was demonstrated was not Job's accomplishment, it was *My* accomplishment—and I say that because I don't want you or anyone to think that I expect *you* to do great things on your own with your power. Because I understand, I realize you don't have any power; you're born in a sinful world and you just don't have power to do good. But you *do* have the power to let Me work in you to do good. Job used his power of choice to let Me, and he appreciated Me, and he gave Me access to his heart. And so it was accomplished.

All down through the ages I have, of course, been working with *whoever* would *let Me* work with them. There have been times when it was necessary to allow a demonstration of what I was able to accomplish in a person or a group of people. And there will yet be times like that. So I will choose people in whom I know their heart surgery has progressed enough so that they're strong enough to stand in the midst of great difficulty, and the demonstration will be vivid and commanding.

There are also times, though, when I choose to allow trials to come on people when I know they will fail. One of the clearest is when Jesus was on Earth with the disciples and Jesus knew the trial and crucifixion were soon to come. He told the disciples, "You are all going to forsake Me tonight." He told them ahead of time. He knew what was going to happen.

He took them to Gethsemane and He invited them to pray, which if they used that time wisely a strength *was* available. I could have done some more heart surgery with them that night. It would have given them the strength they needed to stand with Christ through the trial, which would've been a great encouragement to Him. But, they didn't. They didn't allow Me to do that. They were so disturbed by seeing their Lord and Master weak and falling and just under severe distress, they sought refuge in sleep. And so they missed the opportunity—and *they failed* when the test came. Peter, more dramatically than the others, but all of them failed. And…I allowed that because they needed to see that they were not the great and wonderfully dedicated followers that they thought they were. They needed to see that they were weak, sin-proned human beings like anyone else, and that their only strength could come from relying on Me, depending on Me. It was a hard lesson to learn—but they did learn it. They had to learn it that way, and it was the only way to reach them, and they did learn. As a result, many people who go back and study that learn the same lesson, *not* the hard way, but by learning from the experiences of the disciples.

So, there are those times where I recognize that the test will be failed, but it's not an ultimate failure; it's just a temporary failure or a short term failure that they can learn from and go on to long term, indeed, eternal victory. So, there are both those kinds of tests. You may not always recognize which one is which, but I hope you've seen enough of the evidence I've provided to know that I'm not out to lose anyone—not one. And I…I'm not going to be sloppy about what I allow into your life or anyone else's. I'm working carefully. I'm working in regard to your freedom, respecting it always. And I will always be careful with you. I will always be careful with you.

Female, 36, Nurse, Doha, Qatar:
Dear God, Israel is so small – how have they survived this long?

There is a proverb that says, "Good things come in small packages," which points to the concept that something doesn't have to be big to be valuable. It can be small like a diamond, or a super computer chip, something like that. So the size of Israel doesn't determine its value and its importance and its durability.

The value of Israel at its beginning was tied with the purposes, the *goals* that I had for this nation that would bear to the world the clearest truth about Myself that had been given and would be given before I would actually come to Earth in the person of Jesus. I intended that not only in the teachings and the religious practices of Israel, but even in their economics, their civil laws, their health and dietary practices, hygienic practices, education...really in every aspect of their life, the other nations of the world who would come would be able to observe and learn about Me. People would discover Me in *all* of those things that they would see in Israel. And *that* is perhaps the most valuable thing in all the world—that people would be able to understand Me a great deal better, and therefore, be able to trust Me a great deal more, so that I could bring healing and salvation to a great deal more people, people from every nation and race. Yes, that was the purpose that I had.

However, the leaders of Israel did not allow Me to fulfill that purpose. I should say, they didn't *cooperate* with that purpose. And, I wasn't going to force it on them. And then even when Jesus appeared and sought to give them a whole new opportunity to both know Me and make Me known, they refused cooperation with Him, too, and His ambassadors. But, even after that, *I have not turned My back on Israel,* but have longed to be able to win the respect and understanding and trust of individuals from that group of people. Because they do have a heritage of Abraham and the other patriarchs and prophets, I especially love the opportunity to win them to knowing Me better and really trust Me and to accept and grow from the truth that Jesus presented.

Therefore, I have had My hand upon Israel in certain ways. And, I am still planning to do *a mighty work* among them and to help it so that many will respond to the picture of Me that is seen in both the Hebrew Scriptures and in what Jesus portrayed here on Earth. And that there will be this large group who will then be able, not only to love Me and trust Me, but be able to *reflect* My character to the world so that they can be part of *one last great thrust of light* about Me to the world. And so, I want them there for that, and I'm looking forward to the reality of that, of their participation and *the success that will result.*

Female, 39, Omaha, Nebraska:
Dear God… How do You feel about the attempts at human Cloning?

Because of sin—and remember, sin is lawlessness (1 John 3:4). It's an attitude that says, "I'm going to do what I want to do, and I don't care what the results are or who I'm offending, or what laws I'm breaking in doing what I want to do." And because of sin, man often has an incorrect, a limited, or warped perspective on things.

One of the things that modern man is becoming more and more off track about is his perspective on the sanctity of life.

Because modern man has turned away from believing in *a creator*—and it's interesting to Me that so many can consider themselves religious people, and even Christians, and they believe that I exist and that they can pray to Me, and so on, but they don't believe that *I'm the Creator.* They put their faith in evolution, instead, when it comes to the existence of things. But, because of that, people are losing the sense that life is something to be held as sacred, something that only God can create, and only God should destroy. And therefore man is allowing himself to get more and more into the areas of the creation of life—the formation of a developing human—of trying to choose things that *the Creator* should be choosing.

This is very dangerous ground to tread on.

I told Moses, when he came near to Me at the burning bush, "Take off your shoes, for the ground on which you stand is Holy ground."

I plea to modern man to regain a sense of *what is Holy*. And then, take off your shoes. Don't step where you shouldn't be stepping. You have no idea of the results that can come.

Male, 46, South Bend, Indiana:
Dear God—what do You think of the anti-war protestors?

Well, the anti-war protestors are *people*, and I love people. It doesn't matter who they are or what country they're from or what language they speak or color they're skin or how old or how young. I love people, and anti-war protestors are people. And I think of them as My children, as My friends, as possibly, people that I can enjoy for eternity, and people who can reflect My love and the righteousness of My ways and can be shining examples of how I can save people from a world of sin and selfishness, make them new, and let them enjoy freedom and love for eternity.

Now, your question seems to be directed more

towards their *actions* as anti-war protestors. So, what do I think of people protesting war? Well, it goes back to motives. As I told Samuel the prophet, "While man looks on the outward appearance I look on the heart." That's still true today. So there may be people who are protesting war on the outside but on the inside they have not given up war-like attitudes themselves...in their own homes they're fighting with their spouses or their children or their in-laws or their neighbors, or maybe at work they're fighting for promotions. Or maybe in their anti-war protesting they're fighting for their opinion to be considered or to be dominant. And so they still have a fighting attitude, a motive of trying to be above others. Thus, in a sense, they would not be anti-war at all. Or, maybe they're anti-war because they're afraid of what it will do to their own situations, their own physical well being. For instance, there are Africans who are saying they're against the war because it's going to ruin the economy of their country in Africa. There are Turks who are against the war because they're afraid that the war will spill over into their country and there will be physical harm that will come to themselves and their society. As you can see, there is not just one motive for being anti-war.

Now, if someone is anti-war because they are truly concerned for human life and the well being of others because they realize that war is truly a terrible experience for everyone involved, or because they have a sense of sanctity for human life and that no human should take the life of another, then those motives are more noble, are more in line with My unselfish ways, the law of unselfish love. I appreciate that there are humans who are in tune with that, who are striving for those convictions to be *heard* and to make a difference.

In Jesus' sermon on the mount, He said, "Blessed are the peacemakers." And that indicates My attitude towards those who are protesting war in order to *make* peace, people who are truly lovers of peace, people who feel that *there's power in peace* and in the efforts to preserve peace and to hold up peace as a great ideal condition of world society. And, in the same way, when Jesus finished talking about the blessings on the peacemakers and the meek and so on, He concluded, "Blessed are you when men shall revile you and persecute you." Peacemakers will be persecuted, and certainly those who are protesting war are mocked or ridiculed or even persecuted in some situations. Jesus said that since the world did not accept Him and they persecuted Him they would persecute those who follow in His ways…and that is still true.

Just as there are mixed motives among the anti-war protestors so are there mixed motives among those who persecute them. So we should've called them *pro*-war protestors. Some are pro-war because they truly believe that it's only the threat of war, or the very act of war, that will cause some world leaders, some governments to forsake their plans or actions that are either directly causing harm to others or have huge potential for causing harm to others. These people truly feel that the only way to avoid the ultimate destruction, the destruction of *many* in the future, is to have a limited war with the precise objective of stopping that which would cause hurt later on. But then of course there are those with different motives who simply enjoy war, who want to be part of fighting and conquering. And then there are those who love war because it's just their ambition; they want to advance their careers in the military or they just hate others and want to hurt those whom they hate. So I'm not looking at just the outward appearance of pro-war people, either.

What I would really love to see would be for those who are for the war and those who are against the war to be able to talk together and to share their ideas without the hatred, the animosity coming forth and taking over and causing communication to break down. And, both sides have really made the mistake of not remembering that I am here and I am ready for them to turn to and to trust in. And they don't have to push forward their agendas and be so intent in making them succeed. I've said several times in My Word that I put up kings and I take them down. They can look to Me to do that and trust in Me to guide in the affairs of the world. And I'm certainly here, not only *ready* to do that, but already *involved* in doing it and I'm ready to receive people who want to learn from Me, who want to trust in Me and to cooperate with what My plans are.

Jesus was a peacemaker, certainly, but He didn't put His efforts into protesting wars, He put His time and energy rather into helping people and being loving and spreading the message of love to others. So, I would encourage people to do that, to follow that example. Trust Me, follow the example of Jesus and watch Me work. And I am ready to work—in some big ways. You're going to be surprised at those big ways.

Female, 34, Firefighter, Cape Canaveral, Florida:
Dear God,
In regards to the Columbia Space Shuttle… How do You feel about us humans doing space travel to the moon and "exploring space" in general? And what can You tell us about the Columbia Space Shuttle tragedy?

In general, I think space exploration is very commendable. You know I value freedom and I value individuality of people and I think it's great that human beings have curious minds. I'm glad that you want to learn more, you want to investigate that which you don't know, and you enjoy exploration of almost every kind—especially exploring My creation. I'm excited that there's that interest. And, while I know that there are many who don't have Me in mind when they're exploring My creation, whether it's out in space or in the depths of the sea or with a microscope, still they're exploring My handiwork...and *that* is great to Me. Maybe those who are artists get a little sense of this in that they like to have people examine and appreciate their work. But beyond that, not just that they're looking at what I have made and can be fascinated with the things that I have designed...but the fact that they *want to know more*, and that's something that I intend to encourage all through eternity.

Too often people have a picture of heaven or eternal life as just sitting around doing nothing, like the picture of sitting on a cloud strumming a harp, or just walking around and talking and shooting the breeze but not really accomplishing anything, not really learning anything. Well that's not it—that's a far cry from what I have in mind. I want to *encourage* investigation, and there's going to be opportunity to go through the universe and to learn all kinds of things, and see, and explore things you never even thought of. So, for mankind to be doing that now, that exploration...that's fine. And especially the space program that America has and with which some other countries are involved. They're incorporating the testing of various scientific research theories and materials and so on which can only be tested in space, and that enhances life *on* Earth with various medicines and materials and improvements, and *that* I see as a good thing. So, I'm glad to encourage it.

Now, you speak of the tragedy of those in the Columbia Shuttle, and indeed it is a tragedy. Whenever human beings die it is a tragedy. A sudden death at a fairly young age... I don't regard death coming to an older person, who is feeble and ready to rest until the coming of Jesus, that's not a tragedy; for many it is a relief. But for those young astronauts with so much potential and so many good things already happening in their lives, not just in their exploration but in their home lives, in their education, training and so on... That is a tragedy. And I know that the families hurt and friends hurt, co-workers and all, and I hurt with them. But, that is...again, the part of this great experiment of sin that Adam and Eve chose to allow on planet Earth. Death comes—and that was My warning, that if they chose this, death would come. And it comes not only to the rebellious, the wicked, those who embrace evil, but it comes to the *innocent*, it comes to the good—and so, it has come to the astronauts.

There are dangers in the world and special dangers associated with explorations of all kinds. I am glad to be able to inspire people who are involved with exploration to think of ways to limit the risks and protect the people involved as much as possible. Thus many disasters are averted. Many accidents never take place because of the knowledge and techniques that I'm glad to inspire these people to include in their plans. But, I...I have to allow freedom, and so I don't control everything. I don't prevent all accidents and all tragedies. And this...is one of those. Of course there are innocent, productive, exceptional men and women, girls and boys who are killed everyday in automobile, airplane, and other accidents, fires and illnesses...that happens everyday. I know you don't see it all, but I do. Just as you may be hurting because of seven people who have died, I'm hurting everyday for the *many* whose lives come to an end each day. And I am so much looking forward to the day when there will be no more accidents, no more tragedies, no more death. I want that to be soon. And it will be.

Male, 37, Hairdresser, Hollywood, CA:
God, what is happening with all of this trouble in the Middle East?

Well, you may know that the Middle East is part of the world that I've been very *active* in. I've been active in *every* part of the world, I'm interested in every people from every time period and I've tried to reach everyone. But, in the Middle East I've been able to be more active than other places because there have been some people who responded *more* to what I've been trying to do and how I have been trying to reach them with My thoughts, My ideas and My revelation of Myself. We can go back to Abraham, for instance. He was one who was willing to listen to Me when there was almost nobody else and I was able to teach him a great deal and do a lot with him. We worked together well. Then his decendents down through the ages, especially David and the prophets. And not only with Israel, I was trying to work with other nations as well. The book of Daniel talks about how I was working even with Babylon, a sworn enemy of Israel…and Nebuchabnezar, the king. So, because Israel was there and they were a group of people willing to interact with Me and believe in Me and trust Me and record the things that I was doing there and the information that I shared with them, they had this precious knowledge of Me. So, that's where I was trying to work and bring other people in contact with the correct knowledge of Me. Of course, I'm not the only one working in this world; there's *Satan* and the forces of evil working against what I'm trying to do. He is working in the Middle East strongly, too, and has been through the centuries. Even though now the Christian church is the group of people that I'm able to work the best because they've taken the written material from Israel, which is called the Old Testament, and then they have not only preserved it but have been receptive to the other things I've given, which is now called the New Testament…especially the records of God the Son, called the Gospels. All of that the Christian church now preserves and shares with whoever will listen, and so I'm working primarily through the church in the world.

However, the Middle East still has interest because people all over the world who are reading the Bible and know the history of Israel, realize that's the place where Jesus was, that's the place where

Abraham and David were, and they know that Israel, as a people, were the people I was working through, and so, there is *that* interest. And the various prophecies that I mentioned there in the Bible—people wonder about how some of these things will be fulfilled and *maybe* fulfilled right there in the Middle East. So Satan, with his efforts to confuse people, distract them from the truth and the really important issues *of* truth…he loves to stir up things there in the Middle East. He loves to stir up hatred against the Jewish people because he knows that I really hold the Israelis as dear to Me because of their ancestry, the way that I've been able to work with Israel in the past, and I look forward to a time when there will be many among the Jewish people in the world who will yet respond and accept more of the truth about Me. Satan loves to try to get *at* the Jewish people and cause trouble for them. Also, he likes to stir up things that might be interpreted as a fulfillment of one of the prophecies, to get people worked up about that and distracted from more central and more important issues. But, basically, wherever Satan can cause strife and hatred, warring and death, he'll do it. He does it in all the different countries and wherever he can. There are struggles between Pakistan and India, between North and South Korea, in Ireland, even within parts of the United States—between neighbors, between church members—wherever he can cause strife he's going to do it. Because of the history there, he just has a lot more to work with. This again is part of the effect of having a world where sin is working itself out. It's going to continue until I put a stop to it. And at the right time, I will. I won't say you can bet on it...I'll say you can count on it. It's for sure. Just as surely as I created the world—just as surely as Jesus came and lived and died and rose again—*I will put an end to sin.*

Anonymous:
Dear God,
Somehow I may have hacked into Your web site by accident (if there is such a thing, You would have to tell me that). Anyway, my computer seems to be able to read not only the questions coming into You, but I'm witnessing Your answers, also. My question is...I have a friend who has connections with a publishing company...and I feel compelled to ask You if You would like me to submit these questions and answers to the publisher for their consideration to print into a book that could go out to the rest of the world for many to see?

I certainly don't have a problem with that. As you know, I have inspired many individuals to write down things and compile them into what's called the Holy Bible. And that has been a description of My interaction with this world and has expressed some of My thoughts and feelings and My character and My plans. I have watched over, not only its writing, but the copying of it, and then the printing of it, and the distribution of it around the world in hundreds and hundreds of languages. So I'm glad for people to have as many opportunities as possible to get to know Me. I am not a God who's hiding in the dark; I'm not one who is playing hide and seek with humanity. I'm not standing back waiting for you to come looking for Me, and to try to impress Me with your sincerity or your determination and abilities to look for Me or strive to find Me. I'm reaching after you as human beings. I'm…like the good shepherd Jesus talked about, who goes searching for the lost sheep. And so, I'm glad for anyone who could take things that I've shared with you and share them with others, and the printed form is certainly a good way. So, if you'd like to do that then I'm glad that you want to because, to tell you the truth, I'm the One who has—through the work of the Holy Spirit—I'm the one who put that idea in your head in the first place…and, I'm glad you were listening and that you were willing to respond positively and are ready to push forward with the idea. I can see us working together very well. I have some other things in mind for you—I'm not going to share them with you right now…it will be at the right time. But there's a whole lot we can do together. Just keep listening. I'm right here.

Dear Questioners,

Now I have a question for *you*. When are you going to start taking Me seriously? When will you really look at all the evidence I have given you of My goodness? When will you appreciate the great love I have for you? When will you let go of all the things of your world that soon pass away and accept the abundant life I have for you, which will last forever?

Thanks for opening up to Me and asking your questions. I hope you will come to Me again. I'll be here and I have much more to share with you.

Yours truly,
God

If you have a question that you would like to have answered and possibly see featured in a future volume of **god-line.com** log onto www.god-line.com type in your question and push **send**. Or, e-mail your questions or comments to: questions@god-line.com

god-line.com
The world's questions—answered.